PURPLE CHURCH

PURPLE CHURCH

Starner Jones

Texas Review Press
Huntsville, Texas

Printed in the United States of America

FIRST EDITION, 2012
Requests for permission to reproduce material from this work should be sent to:

Permissions
Texas Review Press
English Department
Sam Houston State University
Huntsville, TX 77341-2146

Author statement: This is a work of fiction, and any resemblance of characters to real persons, living or dead, is entirely coincidental.

Acknowledgments:

This novel would not have been written without the influence of a few people to whom I am permanently indebted. First, to John Reishman, my English professor at Sewanee, who cultivated my interest in literature and composition and taught me how to write. Second, to Herbert Wentz, my mentor of another kind, whose lectures on a quiet mountain in Tennessee still echo in my head, and whose reflections on faith and doubt inform my own. Next, to Jane Lettes, George Core, Patsy Patterson, and Eric Williamson, who edited my work; and, finally, to Henderson Jones, Chris Wiltse, Brandon Shely, and Debbie and Mike Richmond, whose inspiration motivated me to finish the novel and came in the form of these simple yet brilliant words: "Heroes don't die." —Starner Jones

Cover painting by Debbie Richmond
Author cover photo by Courtney Cartwright
Cover design by Nancy Parsons, Graphic Design Group

Library of Congress Cataloging-in-Publication Data

Jones, Starner, 1976-
Purple church / Starner Jones.
p. cm.
ISBN 978-1-933896-89-2 (pbk. : alk. paper) -- ISBN 978-1-933896-92-2 (cloth : alk. paper)
1. Clergy--Fiction. 2. Women college students--Fiction. 3. Memphis (Tenn.)--Fiction. I. Title.
PS3610.O62865P87 2012
813'.6--dc23

2012014025

To the only woman I have ever loved.

Contents

Hope is an instinct
only the reasoning human mind can kill.

—Graham Greene,
The Power and the Glory

PURPLE CHURCH

PART ONE

SCENES FROM HOME

I

Mr. White left open the sturdy door of his red brick tool shed and went out to work the summer garden in his backyard. Somewhere in the distance church bells rang an altar call; the sound echoed across a hollow. A grey squirrel scampered up an oak tree older than time. Long shadows shifted subtly beneath its boughs. Another Sunday was almost gone.

Next door, on a worn yard the old man mowed for free, a group of school boys played baseball and kept score in the dirt. Home plate was a brown paper sack marked with small shoe prints. Third base was etched with a stick. A tireless mother called her sons for supper. Her hands were clean, the apron neatly tied. The young woman's voice came from a white frame house; her command was strong, maternal. A song bird chirped by the kitchen window. It was an idyllic scene, fit for a glossy postcard. The smell of fresh honeysuckle passed through the air.

"Batter up!" one of the boys cried.

Mr. White remembered his youth.

"Bet you can't hit my curve ball!" The batter dug his shoes into the dirt next to home plate.

The old man swiped at a mosquito. It was the first one he had missed that year. His tired feet passed the same antique pickup each time he tended the peas and carrots. He planted them beside each other. "They belong together," he muttered to himself, "Like an ace's curve ball when it's three-and-two."

The mother's clear voice called again as she poured freshly brewed tea into a Mason jar filled with ice at one end of the table. A plank on the hardwood floor moved faintly, not making a sound. The lazy sun cast its last few rays through the kitchen window at close of day.

He picked up a baseball that came to rest in the row of bell peppers in front of him. The scene was from his boyhood. He peered at the ball–its faded seams were like wrinkles on his face. Tiny green marks dotted the ball. Kudzu consumes over time; its stain does not wash off. The wind blew a scent of raw vegetables.

Their game will end shortly, he thought. Mr. White tossed the baseball back to the boys. *So will mine.* The old man knelt beside the green peppers. He looked at the boys, then bowed his head as though in prayer.

A church tower in town pealed seven o'clock. The final stanza was sung by a choir. A song leader lowered his voice at the Baptist church; evening service drew to a close. The head deacon said, "Amen."

"Thanks, Mr. White. Did you see my last home run?" The question was posed with eyes full of life. A trucker shifted the gears of his rig on

Highway 6. The boy returned to the game before his neighbor could answer.

The old man grimaced with pain in his back as he stood. He had not aged well. Gaunt hair on his head lay messily to one side. He had no one to look after him. His wife had been diagnosed with cancer some time ago. She loved him, helped him, but was now gone. He reached for his lower back: tense muscles ached from a strain when they were young. Now age was upon him. Huge feet throbbed under the weight of a thick frame; his broad shoulders carried every burden. In Normandy he fought so others did not have to. A lazy mosquito buzzed past his ear. The summer air was sticky and damp. The old man missed again.

A trickle of sweat made its way along one of the furrows on his old leathery cheek. A calloused hand reached for a kerchief to wipe the heavy brow. Here was a man made weary by years; his struggle with life was nearly over. He frowned once more from pain. In his face was the languid soul of mortal man. The church bells rang softer now that he was old. Brother Jimmy's most recent sermon echoed in his mind: *There is nothing new under the sun.*

Mr. White noticed the first hint of red on the tomatoes as he made his way to the next row in the garden. Soon they would reach their expected hue. Lord willing, he would live to eat again. He savored every bite. In years past he staked the knee-high plants carefully and waited. This season was no different. "Give it time," he whispered. A tattered rag wiped the tough skin on the back of his neck.

Pretty soon I'll be like that truck, he thought, *too old and worn out to crank.* The old Ford had not run in years. Standing there, comforted by the place he knew so well, the sun began to set; its path he saw without looking. It would rise again–whether he saw it or not–only to set once more.

When I die, people will just pass by. He looked at the pickup. *Let me rest in peace.*

A drop of sweat fell on a tomato and took on a shade of red he had seen a hundred times before. He picked one of the plump fruits and took a bite. *Mmmm.* It was the taste of life hanging on, for now. A bit of juice ran down his ample chin. His stout hand closed around the remaining part; a wide mouth followed suit. Mr. White surveyed his garden. His eyelids moved slowly at dusk. Time was an assertive parent watching over a vulnerable child. Death follows the first futile attempt at harvest. His turn was coming.

He sang to himself the lines of a hymn:

I heard an old, old story,
How a Savior came from glory.

Life's beginning and end mark time and *not* the other way about. Some memories fade as years advance; others never do. We bow to Father Time, who with a cool hand delivers more years to us all. Despair finds its limit in death. We know not the hour or place. Like the steady pull of gravity on sand flowing through the thinnest part of a short hour glass, time has its way with our lives. The force tugs souls closer to God knows where and it seems we cannot stop it.

Mr. White leaned to one side as he stood in the garden. He looked at a tomato plant staked in front of him. The work was *his* doing. He tasted a bead of sweat, then blew at the next one. The old man was comforted by routine–daily chores reminded him of his departed bride. They lived contentedly together for many years. She loved him, fed him, then died. Tears blurred his vision as he remembered his dear wife's gentle touch. The best part of him passed with her. He closed his eyes and saw her face. The church bells tolled again, quieter than before. His wife was not around to sing in the choir. He loved her until death–no, he *still* did.

Patience was a natural tendency no hardship could ever vanquish. Clarence White had the patience of Job–nothing lost, nothing gained. He faced the struggle of every man whose greatest enemy was time. The old man would let go of names and faces he loved, but not hope–for hope, his hope, was in his soul.

Farther along we'll know all about it,
Farther along we'll understand why.
Cheer up my brother, live in the sunshine.
We'll understand it, all by and by.

Mr. White observed another Lord's Day. It was proper to do so.

II

The house was occupied by our kin for more than a century. My grandmother was born there. Her mother and brother died there. The place was more than a house, more than an address–it was *home*–and there is no place like it. Come home with me. Be reminded of yours.

In our front yard were three magnolia trees. The largest on the right was my favorite. It was tall, but its lower limbs were smooth and easy to climb. I remember those stiff green leaves and how my small hands disappeared effortlessly behind them during a much anticipated ascent. I remember the sweet sound made as they rustled against each other when stirred by a gentle breeze, and how strong the leaves felt against my bare legs when I perched on a limb in the summertime. They were the biggest leaves I have ever seen and the most resilient, too. Fold them as many times as you want, they still reopen. Our forbears' choice of a state flower must have been easy to make. At least they got *something* right.

On a clear day, from the highest limb of my favorite magnolia, I could see the rooftops in downtown Pontotoc and the statue of a brave rebel soldier standing confidently atop the Civil War monument in the center of the courthouse square. The memorial is dedicated to the sober memory of his valiant service and to honor the courageous sacrifice of countless others just like him. Up close the shrine looked faded and gray–like a Confederate Army uniform donned by Johnny Reb himself–but from a distance, under the South's brightest sun, it looked pure white, radiant as an angel's wings. The soldier's purpose is upright and clear. A small-minded few ignore his epic stand, disapprove of his noble cause. He looks north, from whence the enemy came, a bold rebel willing to fight. The artist knew what he was doing.

Like politicians the monument appears entirely different from a few feet away–less imposing, less severe–an assembly of coarse etches, each deeply personal, distinctively chiseled, and planned with care. And so it is with Southerners. Some are inviting, like a mature Southern magnolia bloom. A few remind you of something that went down long before you were thought of, like the poker-faced Confederate soldier lofted high on a pedestal in the heart of a small Southern town. Speak, magnolia. *Ah, the Civil War. It ended 150 years ago, but it happened just last week.*

Mississippians, like the trees boasting our state flower, need plenty of room. Neither would survive long up north. They would either die from lack of space or overcome the surrounding terrain and its people, and thus be outlawed. Ice storms are to magnolia trees as Yankees are to Southerners. Damn them both for coming too often or staying too long. We can tolerate both of them, but not indefinitely. Like preachers, no two Southerners or magnolia blooms look exactly the same. And like magnolia leaves, Southerners have two sides–one is dark and firm, the other soft and light–one never sees both in a single glance. Magnolias grow deeper with time. Put them in a cramped space and they refuse to bloom. Give them plenty of room and sunlight and watch them grow. Leave them alone. They do not require much upkeep to sustain their wondrous blooms. Magnolias take care of themselves and send forth a flower for all to pleasure in when the time is right.

Mississippi *is* a magnolia–beautiful, abundant, striking. Our sprawling white bloom is the envy of all others. Young ones grow old; old ones inspire. The magnolia tree dare not be pruned–

indeed the practice is strictly forbidden–lest the magnolia refuse to tell a story like no one else can, the kind folks remember for a lifetime to inform each generation, the kind my favorite magnolia cannot help but recall.

Come home with me. Reflect on the precariousness of the Deep South's native people in a uniquely rural existence, for its nether lands are nothing if not ambiguous–certain *and* unstable. Ah, but religion nourishes empty souls and informs ignorant minds, justifying evil as, of all things, *good* in disguise. What does not kill you only makes you stronger.

Understand the practical quality of religion, if not its unintended harm–that framework of general ideas fashioned by a self-anointed certitude and affirmed in indisputable terms, through which we peer for a moment at exactly *who* we are, *what* we are, and what we *do*. The self-righteous know and shout it from the hilltop. Peter was the first pope; John the first Baptist. "How else are we to make sense of it all?" they ask suggestively to enlist a pleasing answer. "All things work together for good," a jolly preacher says, his flushed brow oozing sweat.

Relax. No matter how ridiculous the man-made struggle is, or how easily it may resolve through the application of common sense, just remember to do what you have always done and everything will be just fine.

Welcome to Mississippi: A Place You Will Come To Love *and* Hate. In Dixie we are nothing if not religious: Absurd? Perhaps. Damned? Maybe. Religious? Indeed.

We worship indoors and out, during the light of day and at night. Play fair. Be polite. Live in the moment: the Rebel dream will come true. The lifelong ceremony pervades every facet of Southern life and continues on Saturdays in the fall in a wide-open space known popularly as the Grove. Its sprawling oak limbs connect stately halls to a historic field where fierce battles are won or lost. Families attend lavish parties fashioned in their Sunday best. They march across a tall bridge that once reached over the railroad track and past a magnolia in Hilgard Cut to join loved ones in a spot they rightly call their own. A little girl in a white cotton dress holds her father's hand while they cross the street to enter the heart of the bustling Grove. Her tressled hair is adorned with a bright red bow. Worn dirt paths wind through the idyllic green beneath a canopy of ancient white oaks to arrive at happy hour, a birthday party, and a class reunion all rolled into one. Navy blazers, ties, and pretty dresses are the beloved tradition on another important October day. A drummer plays his fitting roll. The growing crowd begins to cheer.

Are you ready?
Hell yes! Damn Right!
Hotty Toddy, Gosh A'mighty,
Who in the hell are we? Hey!
Flim Flam, Bim Bam,
Ole Miss by Damn!

We lived in the space between the Town and the Wood, closer to the latter than the former. Everyone knew everyone. Residents smiled pleasantly at street dances held in front of the court house steps. A Confederate soldier watched stoically from on high in the middle of town. Ball games drew large crowds when the arch rival paid us a visit, tent revivals too when a handsome young preacher was invited to speak. On Sunday mornings the faithful voiced impassioned and unrehearsed petitions to their Maker in many a country church. We were unassuming if not lowly people–all 5,347 of us–but there was dignity in the way we lived.

We were simple country folk way down in Dixie and far more content with our simple lives of varied hardships than the selfish rich and famous were in theirs. Hard work was an end unto itself. To be blessed was to struggle and do without. Suddenly I feel nostalgic–homesick–far from my family and rural hill country town, a pastoral venue blessed with meth labs and cursed by a shameful history that will not die. Sometimes I wonder how I can still miss that place.

III

Life is a school from which all of us graduate. No one receives an incomplete. Everyone finishes in due course. There is no remediation, no second chance. Upon completion, you cannot push a button and try again. Life and death have a competing cadence–a predictable, sequential rhythm–like the beating of a drum or the timing of a church bell one learns to count on and cannot ignore. We go on to God-knows-where, never to return. Eternity is the absence of time. It has no scale, no dimension. It is *forever.*

Mother Nature rules with an impartial calculating fist. Somber yet fierce, she is poised and deliberate. Unforgiving. As a cheap whore lacking in mercy, she kills for survival *and* for sport, whips the defiant into submission. Like it or not, you will obey. No one ever said the old broad was fair. Who pissed her off this time? Better hope it was not you.

Several years have come and gone since my first comprehension of death and its cold, disrespectful, and untimely intrusion, but I remember the experience as though it happened yesterday. The passing of loved ones has a scripted meaning. Memories of them linger as the smell of a lawn that has just been mowed on the hottest day of the year. Death's enduring relevance defines itself. If death, like virginity, is not precious and consequential, then why is the remembrance of it so ghastly unforgettable? Why must death's proper legacy sometimes bring tears?

Clouds are not supposed to twist, not like that. They are not meant to roar either. Whisper, maybe. But they should not rumble to the point of crash and burn. No one saw it coming. Everything happened so fast. Some thought it was the Devil, others thought it was God.

The tornado came from nowhere amidst a dead calm, then moved closer. It was the only time I felt the ground shake. Hound dogs started barking, pacing to and fro. The wind howled among a chorus of snapping pine trees and electric power lines. Shop windows shattered in town. The entire planet moved. Whirling trash and debris slammed onto home plate. Seams on the baseball were rent. Every animal ran for its fleeting life. Finally, the twister was upon us. Was it here to stay? What did it look like?

Speak, magnolia. *A silhouette of destruction.*

"Aaaarrhh!" came the piercing scream of my terrified mother as she pulled brother and me close. We huddled in the dog trot. Mac knelt at my feet. The two of us held onto her for dear life. Seconds stretched into minutes. The tornado loomed directly over us with deafening fury. An antique lamp shattered in an adjacent room. Slats in the walls crashed to the floor. Light bulbs popped with each frantic jolt from a dying power line. Thunder cracked across a grey sky. *The Lord wouldn't let us die this way, not on Sunday*, I thought. The wind howled louder than the second before. *Or would he*?

The tornado spun faster and louder than hell. Mac dug his nails into one of my legs. "As long as I am with Mama, I will be okay." Time outlasted the ill wind's wayward journey going on and on, and so did we. The dark sky lightened. The twister was gone, a war zone remained.

My family walked outside. Mother shook with rage when we found my grandfather lying dead under one of the magnolias in the front yard. His lifeless body was almost home. A tear in his shirtsleeve revealed a tattoo on his right arm. The faded rebel flag spoke loudly when he could not.

Just the other day, I ran across Doctor Rayburn's death note in a tattered folder at home:

> *Called urgently to the home of A.G. Gregory after horrible tornado. Patient found unresponsive with massive head trauma. Findings: Left temporal ecchymosis and skull depression.*

Pulseless. Apneic. Absent corneal reflex. Pupils fixed and dilated. No sign of life. No evidence of struggle. He must have died instantly. Mr. Gregory was pronounced dead at 5:59 p.m. Cause of death: Blunt trauma to head.

The tornado came and went in a matter of minutes, but its effect endures to this day–all because of wind. Without warning the twister left Papa dead and many of our county's hapless people in a veritable wasteland. Here was another struggle for the good ol' boys down South. Some joined the Army just to get away. Who's afraid of war after he has survived a tornado?

Mama relives the awful storm and pledges never to forgive Mother Nature. She says Brother Jimmy's emotional graveside message echoes in her mind for hours on the anniversary of Papa's passing. Bad memories ring as loudly as the curious sound only a funnel cloud makes when leaving death in its tracks.

A cruel dry spell ensued to mark the last year of my grandfather's life and scorned expectations of a good cotton harvest in Pontotoc County. Most of the cotton was lost in the tornado; the rest perished from dehydration in the mocking drought that followed. But the day a tornado swept across our town and killed my grandfather, it was windy, it was Hell on Earth.

Beware the calm that precedes bad weather. Like a fitly spoken prayer uttered just before a long-awaited meal, it does not last long. *Hallelujah! Amen.*

My family withstood continuous apprehension because of Papa's indiscretions. Now, with the expenses of his burial, money was tight. Our distress remained long after his drunkenness washed out with time and embalming fluid. In death he gave up the bottle. A dead man cannot drink, has no use for the stuff. Papa had his fill; finally–and not a minute too soon–the wait ended. Death called and, boy, did he answer.

Papa was never much for temperance, especially with whiskey or women; at last, intemperance cost him his dismal life. Ah, but he set an unforgettable example, albeit a bad one, for his family not to follow: too much of a good thing reduces the whole. And in my life I have witnessed how extremes undermine life's natural ebb and flow–when one more word ruins a perfect story, when one more step wrecks a smooth dance, when one more note alters a melodiously crafted tune, when one more drink spoils a good night.

Grandma's efforts to constrain him failed, and though all four children tried repeatedly, none of them persuaded him to quit drinking or listen to Brother Jimmy at church. We all have our crosses to bear. The bottle was his and one Papa simply could not carry. He drank every day. Up went the bottle and down went the man. He died the way he lived: drunk and ready for another drink. Papa was a proud and prejudiced man, the poster child of malnourished alcoholics, full of crass one-liners about *colored people*. Mother says he rambled for hours when intoxicated.

"Why did God make Negroes stink?" he asked rhetorically, as he reached for a bottle. "So blind people could hate them, too." Racism amuses the simple.

"Lynchings were common in my day," his rant continued. "But only for people who earned them, I think." He looked away with the blank stare of an unscrupulous child. "There's good niggers and bad niggers, see." That was his conclusion about the entire black race. The distinction was his to make.

A.G. Gregory, 73, died May 24, 1982, at home. Services are 2:00 p.m. tomorrow at Browning Funeral Home in Pontotoc with Reverend Jimmy Russell officiating. Visitation is 5:00 - 9:00 p.m. today. Burial will be in Pontotoc City Cemetery.

Mr. Gregory was a native of Amory and moved to Pontotoc when he was a boy. He was a railroad engineer for many years and the owner of Gregory and Sons Insurance Agency, Inc. until 1975.

Survivors include daughter, Linda of Pontotoc; sons, Steve of Fulton; Grant, a minister, of Kosciusko; Joe of Oxford; sister, Peggy of Tampa, Fla.; numerous cousins; and eight grandchildren.

In lieu of flowers, the family requests that memorials be made to the NAACP of Tupelo.

IV

I hardly knew my grandfathers. Only once was I alone with either of them, and that was in the sweltering viewing parlor at Browning

Funeral Home the evening before Papa's funeral during the last week of May 1982. In those days it was common for country people to sit with their deceased relative during the night before a funeral, and I stayed close to mine until long past midnight, but I never looked at him. Rich city dwellers have last rites, poor country folk a vigil. More than a solemn act, it is a ritual, a rite-of-passage for the living as well as the dead.

Dark clouds emptied themselves as friends and family of the deceased cried tear after tear. Mourning was a second-rate cruise where all on board a small ship felt a constant nausea and swapped places to puke, each time assuring themselves and one another: "This is the last time. No more change in position. No more angst or heart-wrenching tears." But mourning's effectual sickness abates only on the dry land of time.

Grief was the recurrent nemesis everyone failed to avoid. One could not help getting hit with the stuff, and it reeked of an ugly stench–deep, imposing, leaving a permanent stain. Here was another great ocean for more crowded vessels. Wipe the tear away to make room for another. Were they all the same, each a clone of the one before? No, different–like raindrops in a bad thunderstorm–heavy, but never weighing quite the same: this one a symbol of loss, that one a sign of fear, both evidence of internal chaos yearning for order and proof of hurt giving way to healing. Touch them and feel the difference. Go ahead, wipe another. Sorrow, like joy, wanes only with the days we have yet to live.

Closing my eyes, I see mother bereaved over the passing of her father–weeping, not sobbing. Have you ever mourned to the point of pain?

Come home with me. Hear mama cry. Pain is the perception of anguish felt over the loss of someone you can never get back.

Speak, magnolia. *Why cry if you do not hurt?*

Outside Browning the county was soaked. Water was everywhere. The flood rushed for a country mile. Rain fell and fell and fell. Would it ever stop? Were we being punished for someone else's shortcomings, perhaps Papa's unconfessed sins? Maybe God was crying because He could not let Papa into Heaven. Was it dry inside the pearly gates, or was Heaven flooded too?

And what about Hell? Sheol. How was the realm of the dead? Did Papa arrive there yet? *Every knee shall bow. Every tongue confess.*

Anyone heard the forecast from Hell? Ask Lucifer, he will know. "More of the same: Humid again. No chance of rain. Cloudy. Very hot and very dark." Taste blasphemy. Feel its flame. Go on, get close. It's getting hotter. Burn, baby, burn. Talk about pain.

The funeral drew nigh. A cloudy sky was stubborn, not wanting to leave. I found a place in sight of Papa's corpse, and from the cool lingering shadow cast on my curious face hidden behind a grey vinyl chair, I heard my mother crying in the receiving line at Browning. Her eyes were moist and swollen. An empty box of tissue lay on its side in the corner chair opposite the one in front of me and facing the dead man. Across the room, Mama sat to weep, burdened by the unshakable memory of our family's troubled past and uncertain future. She blew her nose and apologized. But her distress was really Papa's fault.

The wait was over. At last, the snake died like a family pet everyone wanted to get rid of, but would not cut off. He slithered on the dirt, then stopped to die while no one was looking. Papa was the product of a pit viper and a stray alley cat, a one-of-a-kind wild animal not meant for domestication. He could not be tamed. Like the worst snake bites, his venom remained long after the fangs let go of his prey–it still circulates in our family blood. Worse than a hungry timber rattler, he bit us all and the poison will last until Kingdom Come. Ah, yes, like a best friend who stops by when you hit rock bottom with cheap whiskey at 3:00 a.m., the fatal potion will always be around.

Mr. Browning passed through the receiving line. One of my uncles motioned discreetly and paid him with cash. It costs good money to die, and even more to be buried right.

"I did not know A.G. had a tattoo," he said with a vacant stare. Mama did not answer. Another of my uncles looked up at him with a smirk and raised his sleeve, flaunting his brightly colored tattoo consisting of a naked showgirl turned around and flanked by twin rebel flags. The most tactful explanation would not suffice.

It was the first time I had been in a funeral home and I hated every minute of it. I wandered into the chapel alone. Through a window I saw a bolt of lightning, then came a feral thunderclap. It was entirely too loud. Mother Nature was at it again. The fertile sound was close enough to soil my pants. A fluorescent visage of the risen Christ lit up as bright as day in the stained-glass window of the vestibule. Queue Electric Jesus: *Fiat lux.*

And God said, "Let there be light,"
and there was light.

More rain fell, creating unrelenting clamor on the roof. I wondered how old it was, if its shingles were rotten or ever leaked. A steady shower pounded the funeral home. Mama cried louder than God as she reached for my hand. God and Mother Nature were in a bad mood and I did not know why. Were they married? No, divorced.

Outside Browning, rain fell harder. It was the first storm in months. I walked home alone and went to sleep without eating or speaking to anyone, stopping only to shed my wet clothes. How could a child so young feel so close to death? What kind of life lay ahead and for how long? *Death waits for us all,* I thought with a spirit of isolated discovery. *Even me.*

Speak, magnolia. *And the light shineth in the darkness and the darkness comprehendeth it not.*

I crawled into bed. Mac lay motionless a few feet away. *Oh God,* I thought, *has Brother died too*?

Mama peeped around the door to check on us, humming softly a familiar tune. My ears were almost numb to her faint whisper as I lay safe and sound in the only home I had ever known. The constant hiss of air through a small crack in a window pane temporarily muted my thoughts about the day's events, but still I did not sleep. The sinister end of every man was forever etched in my head.

V

Morning dawned after a restless night. Still drained from visitation and with legs sore from kneeling behind the gloomy vinyl chair, I awoke feeling dirty. A long school year was almost over. Summer vacation would arrive soon, Little League baseball too. No more preseason, no more prissy school teachers crooning with nonstop tedium about the importance of cursive handwriting or the value of the Dewey Decimal System. It was the only day of school I skipped that year. Mama made sure of that.

Mac had taken his place at the table by the time I arrived in the kitchen. We feasted on a generous breakfast Mama made from scratch.

We had almost taken our fill when he claimed the last pancake Mama cooked at my request.

"That's mine," I said with resolve.

"No, it's not," Mac countered with a grin as he reached for the syrup.

"Now, boys," Mama said, seeking to unite the essence of Christian teaching with the height of civil discourse, "what would Jesus have us to do in a situation such as this?"

Mac looked at me with determined repose. "He would let His *brother* have the remaining pancake," I said, staring hard at Mac.

"That's right," Mama answered, her heart touched by passing joy.

"Okay, that's fine," Mac said, harnessing a budding lawyer's timely repeal. "Why don't *you* be Jesus?"

VI

I rejoined the grieving, who comforted themselves with country ham and casseroles provided by friends and neighbors we received at Browning the night before. Sorrow went on. Death stirred what was otherwise a sheltered mind. The visitation wore on like a sickness one could not shake.

"Hey, Carol," Mac said to one of his schoolmates who was clad in her Sunday best and accompanied by her parents to the funeral home.

"What's wrong with your papa?" the little girl asked.

"He's dead," Mac said with a blank expression.

"He's what?" the girl said.

"He died."

"What does *that* mean? Where did he go?" she said with a look of sincerity.

"Mama says he went to a bad place." Mac folded his arms and sat in a chair.

"Is he a ghost?" she asked.

"No," Mac answered. "There's no such thing as ghosts."

"Oh, yes there *is*," the girl replied.

Most of Papa's friends did not show at Browning. The ones who did hardly spoke. Were they aphasic or just too drunk to talk? The Marlboro Man and Jim Beam, whom he counted on for years, seemed a world away. Neither bothered to call or write. What on Earth happened to the rest of Papa's friends? Were they fed up with him too or did they all die together and reunite with Papa in Hell?

"Better your papa died before Mrs. Gregory," one of the neighbors said. "He would've been lost as a goose in a hail storm without her."

"You'll see him again one day," another speculated with false optimism.

Not unless I go to Hell, I thought.

"I'm sorry about your loss" was fitting consolation.

Dr. Rayburn was the last man who came through the miserable line at Browning before Papa's funeral began. "Your papa's in a better place now," he said as he shook my hand.

How did *he* know Papa's whereabouts? Were doctors suddenly granted access to a posh gated-neighborhood in the firmament? Perhaps he really knew, being the last one to touch Papa. No, *that* was the mortician.

"Thank you, Dr. Rayburn," I said as he shook my hand.

His dear wife said, "Go with God, son."

Where is He going? I wondered. *And how do you know the Almighty's imminent destination*?

"Okay," I consented for a trip to God knows where.

Brother Jimmy greeted Mr. White and his granddaughter, who was home from college. The group tarried on a musty rug in the parlor. A good pastor makes time for a chat.

"Hello," the preacher said with a neutral expression as he looked at the young woman.

"Hi, preacher!" She smiled too big. "I'm Ashley." Her cheeks were pink, angelic. She gave him a half-wink. Her soft blue eyes were as cool as the sea. Men, not mortality, were always on her mind. She had no idea her life could end. The cheerful face drew another look. She was the prettiest girl in town. A bit of white powder was smeared above her upper lip. She gently squeezed her nose, then clasped her hands behind a small waist. Mr. White pulled a kerchief from his shirt pocket.

Brother Jimmy stared at her supple lips as they moved over an inviting chin. Her blouse was exceedingly small and red. She might as well have been wearing a nightie. The youthful cheeks were perfectly made. Blood rushed to a new place in his flesh. Able bones awoke for the first time in years. He had seen her once before at a Christmas party; she waved at him while sipping apple cider across the room.

"Oh, yes," Brother Jimmy said. "Your grandfather mentioned your name at prayer meeting last week." The preacher nodded respectfully at the old man. "He said you were having a difficult time finding good work. I trust you are doing better with the search."

Mr. White walked away.

Ashley rolled her eyes. "Yes, I am." She smiled again. Her reply was as he projected. She told men what they wanted to hear. Sorority girls know nothing but aimless banter.

Brother Jimmy inspected her waist and hair. She smiled and winked at him again.

"I found a job I really like," the attractive coed said, "in a place like none you have ever seen." Her eyes danced as she spoke. She made men nervous by her subtle moves.

"Are you home for the summer?" he asked intently. The preacher scanned the front of her blouse again.

"Sure am," she said with an easy smile. "When are you coming to see me?"

The two spoke only to each other. Her smile was not insincere. She offered him another half-wink. Her entire being relied upon men. Flirting was essential if not biologic. The lips looked like the voice they projected. Ashley's face was suited for a glossy cover. Her natural blonde hair was pulled back neatly into a cute pony tail. She was beauty in mint condition.

"Well, I, uhm," He didn't know what to say. What *could* he say? "Uhm, where do you . . .?" His feet shifted on the rug as he stuttered.

"Oh, I work at Babe's." The young woman was suggestive and fearless. She had a look of determination. "Going on three months now. The money is great!" Her rosy lips lied whenever they could. Seduction was a matter of habit. The young waist swayed back and forth. She placed both hands on one hip, then touched him gently on the arm. The young woman's chin moved freely as she spoke. Her feet moved closer to his. Could he still get the urge?

"Oh, that's, well . . . ." His feet moved again. "You know I can't, er, I don't go to those . . . ." He stepped back from her nervously, a pace off the rug.

"Places where sinners are?" she said with an insulting grin.

God never smites the oblivious. They are too blissfully naïve, not ready to die.

The preacher glanced away. Not a living soul in sight. They were as alone as Adam and Eve. Her eyes threw a smug conceit at him. She had been around a time or two. Sin was convenient and fun. Indiscretion was a handy alternative to the restrictive and narrow way. Brother Jimmy did not know. And, moreover, how could he?

Fornication was a practical undertaking, like war–it happened for good reason. She liked her body. Why hide what you live for?

"I better stay away from Babe's," he said with an air of meekness. The dark cherry floor creaked under his stiff new loafers.

"Oh, I think you would like it." She stared into his eyes until he looked away, meeting them in stride when he glanced at her once more as she turned her small hips toward him.

His neck was moist with sweat. The preacher walked into the vestibule, and the young woman followed him there.

"You don't know what you are missing," she said, touching him on the arm. Brother Jimmy stood motionless in the doorway of the vestibule. She reached into his soul and puckered her lips at him seductively before whirling her tight body to walk away.

It was then that Brother Jimmy looked forward to life again, to the prospect of a lovely young coed and what might be. His heart raced with the fury of an impatient crush. She left the parlor with a blown kiss that no one else could see. With his hands clasped gently against his back, he thought, *She has a pretty smile. I wonder how old she is.* The wooden floor moaned again when he took a step on the faded rug in the parlor. *Probably not even legal yet.*

VII

Friends and neighbors who brought food served as pallbearers and uttered more attempts at reassurance. The last to go away took their time in doing so. Why does goodbye take so long?

Our family was left to mourn privately. An uneasy silence came and went as I broke it by saying, so God and everyone else could hear me, "Rest in peace, Papa." Mama reached for my hand. Soon life would return to normal–as soon, that is, as we settled the argument over who would get Papa's seasoned Winchester shotgun, the only valuable item he left behind and that he clearly bequeathed to only one person, *me.*

Following the last verse of "Amazing Grace," the graveside service carried on with the preacher's solemn words. Our family stood at attention. Brother Jimmy held open his Holy Book and read from *Ecclesiastes*:

> *Vanity of vanities, saith the Preacher, vanity of vanities; all is vanity.*
>
> *What profit hath a man of all his labor which he taketh under the sun?*
>
> *One generation passeth away, and another generation cometh; but the earth abideth forever.*

"Let us pray," the preacher said in a somber voice. Sunlight beamed on his freshly shaven face. A small bird sang in the distance. Brother Jimmy bowed his head. Ashley White stood by her grandfather; his face was calm and sure. She looked at the preacher while he prayed.

"Our Father in Heaven," he began without delay, "in your Holy Word you tell us that you have gone to prepare a place for us." Mama wiped another tear and pulled brother and me close. Brother Jimmy prayed with his eyes tightly shut. "Ashes to ashes, dust to dust," he said with care. The prayer concluded with a collective "Amen."

Now for interment.

We looked with disbelief as funeral home employees dropped my grandfather's coffin when it was halfway down the hole. Muddy water splashed from the bottom of the stinking pit and onto mother's beige satin dress. One of the men who lost his grip slipped and fell into the grave.

Mr. Browning questioned his help indiscreetly, "Didn't we replace those rotten straps?"

We stared at the speaker as if he were naked or gay. A man of such wealth and position in town was not expected to speak so carelessly. His status was above what had just happened.

"Didn't we?" he asked again.

Everyone stood in an awkwardly silent abhorrence until one of my uncles answered as though inspired by the Holy Ghost: "Guess not."

Another laborer was just as imprudent with his words, aimed in the direction of my poor mother. "Sorry about your dress, ma'am. That dirt ought to come out in the wash."

You cannot buy class. Like Mother Nature, it is simply not for sale: "Class?" queried the redneck. "Is that with a *c* or *k*?"

Mama rightly ignored him.

We peered at the grave. The head of Papa's coffin lay ajar, revealing part of his dreadfully pale countenance. Here was the mugshot of a wayward man's ugly death.

Speak, magnolia. *Guilty as charged. Never to live again.*

Another uncle tried to shield Mama from

the ashen face, but was too late in positioning himself in front of her. Looking up I heard her wail at the brink of madness. She screamed hysterically as her father's lifeless form rested afloat in the coffin's murky water–all because of wind. She wept the night before while receiving friends next to Papa's corpse at visitation, but this was different. Did she see his soul suffering in Hell? In delirium Mama unwittingly amended a line from a famous novel. Her reference was eerily intimate: "My father is a fish."

VIII

Even with the memory of a deadly tornado and my family's grief over the loss of its shameful patriarch, summer vacation was replete with fun. I remember those warm afternoons spent playing baseball with Mac and the taste of Mama's freshly baked chocolate chip cookies served with a glass of chilled milk. But most of all, I recall with fondness climbing to the top of my favorite magnolia tree and looking out over the hollow that led into town. I remember the story told to me by the sprawling magnolia as I propped my feet leisurely on its highest limb and leaned back against the trunk. I had not a care in the world when the tree spoke its plain wisdom to admonish and warn. Ah, yes, now I remember the faint whisper that came from my eager lips and the timeless story the magnolia told only to me.

Speak, magnolia, then let me go.

For there is nothing hid that shall not be made known.

PART TWO

SOMEWHERE IN MEMPHIS

I

Time passed. The sturdy door of the red brick tool shed remained open. Its color faded like the seams of a baseball left too long in the summer sun. Low limbs of sprawling magnolias sagged like the droopy cheeks of a basset hound. The seasoned monument at the center of court square looked as tired as the cause it remembered. The soldier with his principled expression stood composed and ready.

I got older. Mr. White became older, too. He was always old. Time is the one thing we constantly lose.

"Hey, batter, batter! Swing, batter, batter!"

Swing and a miss.

"Strike one!"

The old man inspected the peppers in his backyard. Deep wrinkles around his eyes were years in their making, a timeline that spanned four score and two.

"Top of the ninth," he muttered. "I must be

on deck by now." His face was the composite of a tired old man. Two hungry hound dogs barked next door. Wearily the old man hoed his summer garden. Sweat dripped from the sagging brow.

Someday those boys will be old like me, he thought. A motorcycle whined on a narrow road close by. The old man looked to the sky. A single puffy cloud faced east toward Heaven. Mr. White reached for a kerchief. The cloud moved slowly overhead. It was a transcendent scene–sublime–fit for a Rockwell inside a pricey custom frame.

That will be my new home. Get to watch the game from there. Listen to the angels sing.

I heard about a mansion
He has built for me in glory.
And I heard about the streets of gold
Beyond the crystal sea.

The bases were loaded.

"Hey, batter, batter! Swing, batter, batter!"

The old man leaned against the rusty pickup resting on concrete blocks and missing two of its wheels. Knee-high weeds surrounded the truck. A mother's voice called from the back porch next door. "Boys, the cookies are ready!"

Swing and a miss.

"Strike two!"

"Come and get'm!" the woman cried.

Life ends before we know it, the old man thought. He looked at the sky. *Only wish I had . . .*

"Hey, batter, batter! Swing, batter, batter!"

The baseball popped again in the catcher's mitt.

. . . more time.

"Strike three! You're out!" the pitcher screamed. The boys ran to the porch of the simple Southern home.

The old man winced from a pain in his lower back. His gilded features stood out like a wide tombstone expressing the last few important words said about a noble man.

One of these days I'll strike out and head for a place of comfort, too. Life's brevity was upon him. *Never to swing again.*

The frailty of mortal man weighed heavily on his mind. His face swelled with feeling. The garden was picturesque. He tended it every day, alone. His sore feet yearned for rest. "Some things are worse than dying," he whispered. There was nothing new under the sun.

Brother Jimmy's sermon echoed softly in his head:

> *To everything there is a season, and a time to every purpose under Heaven.*

His coed granddaughter waved from a distance. The wind gusted suddenly, lifting her short cotton skirt. She walked with her head high. Ashley White lived for a man. Smooth, tan legs looked just like they should. She was wet with desire. The smooth, curvy slit was ripe. Men were always on her mind. Hurriedly, and with a goal in mind, she left for work. Looking up, she saw a pale sky. The forecast called for rain.

A rough wind blew kudzu back and forth, dark clouds loomed overhead. A herd of cattle grazed in a green velvet pasture as the lovely young coed drove north on a perilous two-lane road. The youngest heifer mooed at her last playmate when the first raindrop fell. The court square was empty, save the statue of a tall rebel soldier and the stately magnolias paying homage at his feet.

II

Brother Jimmy passed the idle Monday as he did all the rest. The church office was closed. His day began with scripture and prayer, then continued with a generous breakfast he ate by himself. A framed picture of his bride stood on the counter next to the kitchen sink. The young preacher attended to his late wife's affairs and took his time in doing so. He sat alone on the floor in his bedroom and sorted through her Sunday clothes and pictures from a happier time. The local pantry called for donations whenever their benevolent stock ran low, and the preacher did what he could to assist those in need; helpless souls counted on him.

Tears welled in his eyes as he held a photo of his eventual bride that was taken while she was in college. Her face was pretty and bright. He stared at the picture and cried. She looked good in anything, but the knee-length silk dress that was still neatly pressed in his lap was always her favorite. The preacher wiped a tear from his face. An assortment of her Sunday best was before him; she had shoes for any occasion. The stack of cotton blouses in front of him smelled like her neck and chin. The preacher's mood was tempered a bit. He remembered his faithful wife with cheer. Ochre green was especially appealing on her: It complemented her dark brown hair and olive skin.

A small black book lay in one corner of the closet. Brother Jimmy reached for the diary that was opened near the middle. Every page was neatly penned. His wife's handwriting made him think. With misty eyes and a prayerful heart, he began to read:

September 27, 1981

I was diagnosed with cancer two days ago. The doctor gave me six months to live. Soon I will be dead and gone, unable to look after the vulnerable child. She will be alone again. I pray God will keep her safe. I pray that Jimmy will do what he can, maybe take her in if he marries again.

After that, he read the entire diary from the start–the entries about their first date and kiss on the lips, the trial sermon he was nervous to give in front of a packed house on Easter morning, their honeymoon in the Holy Land and steamy vacation in the Smokies over a long weekend, her diagnosis of leukemia.

March 6, 1979

Thought I was pregnant last week, but it was a false alarm. It would be a miracle if I conceived, but I'm beginning to think such a wondrous act does not happen to gals like me. Jimmy and I have considered adoption. He says we've tried enough to make it happen on our own, but I still think we need to do it more and maybe try a different approach.

Brother Jimmy thought of his late wife's soft hands and supple lips. He remembered her loving embrace. He wanted to taste the stuff of life again and he dreamed of experiencing, once and for all, the beauty of family–Americana in the truest sense of the word–husband, wife, and child in the comfort of a stately home; eating together, talking, laughing, praying together–living the way happy people often do. If only his pretty wife were still alive–her words had the power to heal. He drew a deep breath as a heavy tear fell onto a page.

March 31, 1979

. . . It is hard being a preacher's wife. Everything I do is on record for all to see. At least I am still in love. Jimmy has always been good to me.

April 27, 1979

There is a young girl at church who has confided in me. She says I am a good listener and wants me to be her mom if something ever happens to her real mother. She was very distant at first, but now has gotten quite close. I am not sure how to handle her. She is afraid to be at home and says her father touches her "down there." At first I did not believe her, but she must be telling the truth because her claims are just too real. He goes into her room when her mom is asleep. "My daddy is Satan reincarnated," she told me today, "He is the Devil in a man's body. I am tired of all this."

It seems unfair that I am unable to conceive when a man so evil can get a child with no trouble at all, only so he could molest his precious gift. How can a merciful God permit such evil in the life of a helpless girl? It just isn't fair.

May 25, 1979

I can't stop thinking about little Ashley White. That poor girl. She's so cute. I wish she could live with us. Oh, God, you sent us grace. Give it to her, too. May she know your peace.

August 12, 1979

The young girl's father died last night. This may sound terrible, but I am glad he is gone. I hope Hell is real so he will be punished forever because of what he did to her. Dear God, I wish she could live with us, but what would the people at church say? What would the deacons think? I will give my soul up forever, only let her see Christ through me.

June 28, 1980

Ashley smiled for the first time in months today.

November 30, 1981

> *Sometimes I think of her for no reason at all. It must be the chemo. Last night I dreamed she moved in with us. We tucked her into bed and she said a prayer we had taught her. I felt more like a woman than ever before–with a tender life to nurture and mold, like the devoted mother I can never be.*

Brother Jimmy placed the diary in his lap. *I must witness to her.* He cradled the small black book in his hands. *She needs to feel loved by me. I've got to witness to her, save her, be Christ to her.* His face was determined and sure. "Oh, God, give me strength," he prayed. "Ashley must be saved by You."

She was a well-bred college coed and Delta Delta Delta to the core. "Try Delta," the saying goes: "Everyone else has." Life was easy until her parents died. Her father was a wealthy man and doted on her night and day. Daddy made all the right moves in business when he was young–shook all the best hands. His was a life of comfort and influence. Her mother was president of The Junior League. They were the proud and privileged few until it all came to a tragic end when he flipped his car on the way home from a company board meeting at Perdido Beach, killing himself and Ashley's mother. But life and its games carried on. Her grandparents managed her fine through the teenage years. Life insurance provided them with plenty to raise her, but they were frugal people who walked the straight and narrow.

She was crowned Homecoming Queen and elected captain of the cheerleading squad. She had nice things, pretty and popular friends, and she was experienced enough to know that it felt good, really good, to be someone everybody knew. Ashley treasured her grandparents as a little girl, but now her granny was gone and Clarence White was old. To be sure, her grandfather loved her, but she needed something more. She missed dressing up for pageants while her parents watched and holding shiny trophies over her head. She cared nothing for Sunday school or choir practice or that damned vegetable garden out back, but relished in the production that was her family's tradition on Sunday morning.

Her outing as a slut at the prom ruined any chance of landing any of the boys of better circumstance in town. But after leukemia claimed the life of his loving bride, the handsome young pastor at the Baptist church was eligible again. So, on that fateful night in June, her wallet nearly empty after buying too much coke and expensive perfume, she paid a visit to the preacher's house, then headed north to dance on stage, hell-bent to make a better life.

Brother Jimmy was a hometown boy and finished top in seminary. His mother had a puritanical slant. She pushed him hard as a child in Bible Drill. He studied diligently and shunned distraction, until the Lord called home his loving bride. Still, he carried on in the quiet town and turned the Baptist church on its ear. Attendance: Up 100 percent. Offerings: Up 150 percent. His was a dynamic presence even the Devil could not ignore. Jimmy Russell was born to preach. He was somebody special in town and easy to look at, too. He tasted the good life with his devoted spouse until it all came crashing down. Brother Jimmy had driven the sundry streets of Memphis on his way to Big Baptist when his wife was dying there. He passed the converted warehouse on Winchester many times, but had not thought much of it. The place blended in with the surrounding poverty and despair. *Babe's*, the preacher thought as his hands gripped the wheel, *I wonder what it's like inside.*

Clergymen are vitally important in a small southern town. Acquiring their privileged opinions and knowledge from vicarious experience and holy decree, they relay divine messages, explain calamity, foretell sinister times, and attempt to keep us all in line. Every sermon comes from the heart. Every prayer is fitly said. Their words are baked with conviction and the obligation to secure a place for all souls in the quiet repose of the life hereafter–our appointed destiny that some are sure of, but have never seen.

This is a story of contempt more than grace. The tale reverberates in sober minds and trusting hearts, edging closer and closer to troubled souls. Its lesson is plain: Even good men fall. Sometimes they blame themselves when the bitter end is near, and often they marvel at the lenient tenor of their righteous God, who grants every man the freedom to choose an evil path. Curiosity breeds the fatal step borne of solitude and despair in the lonely man's empty heart. Unwittingly he decides his tragic fate. However innocent, however made, the onerous demise of religious men spawns from a casual glance and ultimately culminates in an irrevocable moral blow. The flattering look and quick embrace usher a forceful tide of shame and reproach. One lapse in judgment and all is lost. A moment of pleasure, entered with haste, may well bring along a lifetime of heartache. Yes, even good men fall–even the widowed Baptist preacher whose manhood wages war with a broken spirit in the darkest recess of his believing heart.

III

Ashley awoke in a fog to the warm sun beaming through a cloudless sky. Across her messy room flies passed in and out of an open window. The frame was too heavy for her to raise–only beefy muscles could move it. Wilted tulips crouched in a clear serpentine vase resting on the dusty sill. The smooth glass was marked with fingerprints, a gift from a forgotten boyfriend who had adored her flesh and bones. The young woman rolled over while she was still half asleep. Pink thong panties were moist in the middle. She thought of Spring Break. An erotic desire made her feel new. There was never enough time. A soft breeze kissed her face; it glowed from a dream she could not recall. A hot shower felt good. She dressed in a hurry.

"Good morning, angel," the old man said as she entered the kitchen with a wobbly gait. "Did you sleep well?" A songbird chirped by the window.

Avoid argument at any cost, she commanded herself. Her fangs were poised for a deadly strike.

Blood rushed in the space behind her eyes. *Stay calm and keep it civil.* She could not wait to leave.

"Yeah." The best answers were reflexive and lean. Did he have to ask? She just needed a place to stay until . . .

"You were late for curfew last night," the old man said.

Silence.

"Maybe it is time you were on your own." Her grandfather was patient and true. The weighty clock in the hallway chimed half past eight.

Just be quiet, she thought. *You can move out as soon as . . . .*

He looked at her from across the room.

"Yeah," she answered curtly. "Maybe so." The young woman slammed the door with a scowl as she left for work.

She arrived somewhere in Memphis. It was her other home–the place where she wanted to be–a gal felt at ease. A lovely coed was welcome there. Business was booming. Damn straight, no one bitched at her. The new girls learned quickly. She strutted with the pride of a reckless wild turkey: "Hands off, Cherry. Those clear heels are mine."

The metal lockers were an unflattering shade of casket grey. The one next to the bathroom door was inscribed with her surname. She kept a stack of photos on the top shelf where no one bothered to look. Her smiling mother on the beach in Destin took her back to an innocent day; the verge of laughter was stuck on her face. *Good times,* she thought, inspecting the picture at the start of day. *Maybe someday I will be happy again.*

On the locker door marked with her last name: "You go girl!" A fake silver cross hung from a hook. She thought all jewelry was cute. Imagery had no bearing in the sexy coed's mind. She had no use for the crucifixion. On the locker next to hers: "Whoop that trick!"

Puberty was her favorite time. She did not mind the hassle, the gory friend who demanded the monthly visit, the bloody rush that scared some men away. She made the most of it. Her body changed for the better, and she made it count in the glowing spotlight of a lofted stage. No, she did not mind her body's change. Her buttocks were hard as a green apple. Her face was perfect. Ashley could see it changing into the kind her mother wanted to see.

She was getting taller; her breasts were fuller. The waistline and youthful hips were now more defined. She was becoming the darling young woman her mother raised her to be: vivacious, charming, wanted by all. She barked the same warning when another Friday night rolled around: "Stand back, girls. High-rollers ask for me."

Dingy steel bars covered each window. The girls were already sentenced. The whole place said, "Stay Out." Giant metal doors were locked to protect them by day. A hired gunman with his weapon concealed guarded the nest after a busy night. Regulars did not bother to stop at the door or flash an ID. Strange men were welcome inside the club; their money counted, too. Babe's never turned any man away, at least not at night.

"Drunk as a bicycle on Sunday at 2:00 a.m.? Sure. Come on in!"

"Divorced and happier than ever before? Welcome to our world."

"Want to get high with the latest gung? Here, try this."

"Ready to get laid tonight? Get your ass in here!"

"What's up, money? Who you tappin' these days?"

"Looking for Tammy, er, I mean Diamond? Too bad, player. She's busy now."

"Sore from an all-night-orgy with Raven and Cherry? So, how was it?"

"Got that smelly discharge, huh? Told you so. Didn't listen, did you? Happened to me, too."

"Hand your keys to the large black man at the front door, gentlemen. It will be the last time you see your car."

"Babe's," read the purple neon sign as it flashed in front of the converted warehouse building, "The Name Says It All."

IV

Stepping into the spacious room, he stared at the stage with raw, expectant eyes as if exploring a foreign country he had never visited before. Nature called when he saw the first half-clothed dancer. He rounded a dark corner by the men's room and took out his penis. He looked sheepishly at the small space around him. Was this how prison felt? The stall in the men's room was covered with graffiti.

Brother Jimmy was filled with shame. "Beware loose women and pickpockets," His conscience growled. This was no gentlemen's club. He looked straight ahead. "Perverts, only, please; they come here to shit." Specks of fecal matter dotted the commode. The bathroom smelled as it looked.

In his face was the gleaming portrait of blasphemy's next convert who if caught with his pants down would immediately recoil. His eyes scanned the graffiti. "We like our women the way we like our bourbon–old enough to drink!" His soul bounced with horror. "Fuck her, stupid. It's good for the heart!" His chest was numb with disgrace. "And soul, too!" someone had added with black ink smeared to one side. His nervous eyes were deliberate.

Scribbled with daring red letters: "Jesus was here." He reached for an ink pen. The Spirit was still in him:

is
Jesus ~~was~~ here. And he weeps for your lost soul.

Clergymen boil when the temperature reaches debauchery. A sour taste oozed in his mouth. Wickedness churned in the his stomach. Nausea surged in his gut. He needed fresh air. Brother Jimmy looked for a piece of soap to wash his hands.

He walked back into the club. With his deliberative face and neatly groomed hair, his manner anxious and tense, anyone could see that he did not belong. The preacher moved with short, choppy steps. He rubbed his eyes as he passed the stage. His athletic build had faded some after the death of his wife. She fed him, took care of him. He took a seat at a corner table. Brother Jimmy was not a VIP.

One of the waitresses moved smoothly to take his drink order. "What'll you have?" the stumpy redhead asked, her face pale from the menstrual state.

"Root beer, please."

The waitress rolled her eyes and turned away. He dared not order a beer.

There was no sign of the lovely coed. Brother Jimmy leaned back in the swivel chair. A dumb jock stepped to the lone microphone on stage. "What's the difference between a hooker and a whore?" he said with a fleeting grin.

"What's that?" someone questioned. The meathead dodged an ink pen hurled by a man wearing a wrinkled dress shirt at the back of the room.

"Yeah, say it!" another cried. A young woman's laughter came from the dressing room.

"Tell us now!" one of the perverts demanded as he reached for his drink.

The comic took a sip of his beer. "About five bucks!" he yelled.

The growing crowd chuckled with approval. Their amusement was vile and insincere. Oh, what the hell? They were among friends. But he was not in the loop. Brother Jimmy was not indifferent to dirty jokes. He saw the graffiti again in his mind. "We like our women like we like our . . . ."

Jesus was here. In a club, of all places, he thought. *How crude.*

The meathead continued, the bill of his baseball cap turned backward. "How do you clean a dirty condom?" The scant audience braced for a hearty punch line. "Turn it inside out and wash the fuck out of it!" The faint sound of cheap laughs reached the front of the stage. A stripper who sat at the bar covered her mouth with one hand as she giggled. One of the bouncers took a sip of his drink.

Brother Jimmy walked outside and drew a deep breath. He flinched when the beaten metal door slammed shut behind him. The patio was empty, save two of the strippers on a smoke break. They talked quietly to each other. The preacher folded his arms against his chest as he looked at one of the girls who ashed her cigarette daintily and whispered something into the other stripper's ear.

"Now the serpent was more subtle than . . . ."

He moved a few steps away from the door. One of the women reached for her handbag and went back into the club. "I'm next on the pole," she said. Her heels popped as she pranced by and flung open the metal door. He looked at the blonde stripper who sat alone primping her hair. Her pink thong was easy to see. The young woman's face looked familiar. He walked toward the stripper with a troubled expression. She turned as he approached. The smell of a burning cigarette almost made him gag. In bold block letters her skinny tee shirt exclaimed: "FUCK YOU, MOTHERFUCKER!"

"Preacher, is that you?" she asked. The metal door slammed shut again. "Well, hell fire! If it isn't Brother Jimmy Russell!" The young woman voiced her surprise with evident zeal. "What brings you to Memphis?"

Brother Jimmy recoiled. His muscles were too slow to answer. His mouth twisted with panic. Humiliation was customary and free–to everyone but the sufferer. He could not speak while he stood, had not practiced his words in a club.

Keep calm and carry on, he thought. Brother

Jimmy spotted an empty chair close to the stripper. His hands were nervous and moist. His head spun to see if other men looked on.

The young woman held a cigarette between her freshly painted nails. “Never thought I’d see the likes of you here. What have you been up to?” she asked with a blazing smile.

He sat across from her at the wrought iron table, kept a safe distance. A cabana umbrella hung over their heads. The air smelled of lit tobacco.

“Please call me Jim,” he said. The preacher’s hips felt sharp on the bare aluminum chair. The young woman cast a familiar half-wink through the steamy air.

“Okay, anything for my hometown’s most eligible man.” Her eyes glistened as they scanned his face.

“You invited me here, remember?” His hands took a firm hold on the space behind his knees.

“I did? Well, okay. Fridays are my best night, so don’t take it personal if I disappear for a minute or two now and then. This place gets pretty wild after eleven or so. Ha! You know what the folks at home say, ‘It ain’t a party if the cops don’t break it up.’ Say, I’ll be on stage in a few. When will I see you in a birthday suit?” She winked at him and crossed her legs that cast a radiant sheen long sought by every man. She took a lengthy drag on her cigarette. A tiny silver cross hung on her chest.

“I like your necklace,” Brother Jimmy said. He tightened his grip on the back of his knees.

She was not an avid follower of Jesus, but at Ole Miss had been known to holler out his name in bed a time or two. Frat boys swear she trekked around campus with a mattress tied to her back. Ashley White could get lucky with anyone. Oxford was saturated with good looking men.

"Oh, thanks," she said. "Say, have you heard the one about the preacher who died and went to Hell?" Ashley leaned forward and straightened her thong in the back.

"No," the preacher said.

"Want to?" She smiled eagerly, not caring what his answer would be.

"Well, I . . . ." He was silenced by her charm.

"A preacher died and went to Hell. When he arrived, the Devil met him at the fiery gate and said, 'Hello and welcome to Hell. I'll show you around.'

"So the Devil took him down a long hallway. It was hot and dark. There was weeping and gnashing of teeth. They came to a door. The Devil flung it open, took a drag from a cigarette, and said, 'Go ahead. Have a look inside.'

"The preacher did as told and saw a beautiful young woman, completely naked, massaging another clergyman's shoulders."

"'Wow! This is all right!' the preacher said. 'I could get used to this!'

"Then the Devil took him to the next door in the long hallway. It was hot and dark. There was weeping and gnashing of teeth. They came to another door. The Devil flung it open, took another drag from his cigarette, and said, 'Go ahead. Have a look inside.'

"The preacher did as told and saw a beautiful young woman, completely naked, kissing and servicing a priest."

"'Wow! This is all right!' the preacher said. 'I could get used to this!'

"So the Devil took him to the next door in the long hallway. It was hot and dark. There was weeping and gnashing of teeth. At last, they came to another door. The Devil flung it open, took a drag from his cigarette, and said, 'Go ahead. Have a look inside.'

"The preacher did as told and saw another man of the cloth having his way with another beautiful young woman, completely naked.

"'Wow! This is all right!' said the preacher. 'I could get used to this!'

"And the Devil said, 'Not so fast, my friend. This is hooker Hell. Preacher Hell is down the hall!'"

V

They moved their strained conversation inside. Brother Jimmy scanned the room instinctively. His manner was careful and taut. A poster by the pool table read: Tap Out Tuesday—Beer Bust All Day. He could not hide the discomfort in his soul. He sensed the people around him laughing inside their heads at his plainly sober expression, his tightly combed hair, the cleanly shaven face, and the clumsy way he walked around the club.

"Ready for a lap dance?" the young woman said with a grin.

"No." He shifted his feet.

"Not until you see me topless, right?" Ashley lifted her shirt slightly in the front. Brother Jimmy drew a whiff of the smoke-filled air. He was nauseated by the scene in front of him. Ashley elbowed him in the ribs. "Loosen up," she pleaded. She introduced her honored guest to Heavy D.

"Nice to meet you." Heavy D offered his hand.

"Jim," the preacher said.

"Pleasure's all mine, sir," Heavy D said. They shook hands and let go quickly. The preacher cleaned his hand behind his back when the bartender turned to pop open a beer.

"First time here, Jimmy?"

"Please call me Jim," the preacher said.

The bartender wiped the counter with a moist rag. He nodded at the preacher as he folded the rag.

"He's a bit shy," Ashley explained as she peeped at a vacant pole on stage. She was jealous of the next gal who would grip it while frustrated men watched with lustful intrigue. Her eyes fell on a tip jar stuffed with crumpled dollar bills.

Heavy D placed a soiled glass in the sink. "Don't sweat it, Jimmy. You're in for a good time at Babe's. Met my best bitch here a few years ago. Hell, you might meet one too if you hang around long enough. This place is full of desperate broads."

Ashley White took her place on a stool. Brother Jimmy did not respond. He knew why he was there.

And the light shineth in the darkness and the darkness comprehended it not.

"Yeah, I've met a couple of gals in here," the bartender said. "The best one, Sheila, now she was an animal. We got a little boy together, two years old. Looks like his old man, huh huh." Heavy D took a gulp of his beer. "You got kids, Jimmy?"

"No." He shifted his feet on the stool.

"Two years old. Said his first cuss word

the other day, huh huh. Hope he gets further in school than his old man." Heavy D tossed an empty can into the trash. "Wouldn't take nothin' for him. His mama left me, though. Cunt." He looked at the clergyman. "Huh huh!"

"Very sorry to hear that," Brother Jimmy said. Ashley giggled and rocked back on the stool.

"Eh, shit happens," Heavy D replied. "She'll be back. There's more than one way to choke to death on butter." He lit a cigarette. "I split with my second wife last week. She worked every weekend for a solid year. Doesn't need the dough as bad anymore, since she finished nursing school." He put down the lighter and reached for an ashtray.

"Must be nice."

Ashley grinned and swung her legs under the bar stool where she sat. A stripper flicked her hair up in the back while walking by. "Hey, Tammy, er, I mean Diamond," she said with a wink. The young woman turned and kissed her friend on the cheek.

"Ah," the bartender said. Fate was paramount. There were no choices in this world, none that really mattered. Heavy D thrived on controversy, however petty, and never mind if it meant rushing to the arch enemy's inane defense. Suitably are the simple so called.

One of the local Negroes pranced into the club wearing a red velvet sports coat decorated with silver sequins, dark blue jeans, brown pointed shoes, and a gold earring. The man was accompanied by his nephew, who could not have been more than twelve years old. The boy had no idea who his father was. Alas, and without fear, his sometime uncle showed him the Memphis way. With his green fedora and dirty nails, anyone could tell the boy felt at home–at home in the club, as in the abandoned warehouse on the corner of Poplar and Third where he took the occasional hit from his uncle's hot crack pipe. The boy nodded at one of the strippers who walked by as he lit a smoke by the bar. A soft vapor emerged from one end of the club. The air smelled of a queer haze. Sounds became louder, the music clearer. Brother Jimmy's eyes opened wide. He had never seen or smelled marijuana.

A black man approached the bar and perched himself on a stool. He made his presence known like a crow that does not shut up.

"Heavy D, let me have a drink on the house. Is it happy hour yet?" The beak wanted for a good cleaning. A fake gold earring hung from his ear: Cat Man. His faded tee shirt was from a large meeting of related Negroes who gathered on a feckless day in the spring.

JACKSON-EVERS FAMILY REUNION
Clarksdale, Miss.
May 17, 1980

He was a faithful loiterer, categorically unemployed, and crooked as a dog's hind leg. He had relinquished the good fight long ago, except as a pusher who sold the imported white powder in the pitch black on Union and First. The man hoped one day to find a dancer with her guard down in the parking lot and rob her of what she had made during a busy night at Babe's.

A chubby English bulldog sat in a corner behind the bar, its jowls drooped like one giant wrinkle. The brown leather collar had the word

Bully on it. The dog barked his answer to the inviting allure of Ashley's designer perfume.

"Easy, Bull," Heavy D said with a foolish grin.

She knelt to pet him under the chin. Brother Jimmy watched with jealous interest. Blood rushed from his head in a moment of lustful release. He needed to be touched, caressed. The bulldog barked again.

"Bully!" Heavy D snapped as he slid the dark patron a beer. The bulldog yawned and licked himself. Ashley White gave her visitor a half-wink and then pinched the preacher in the small of his back. Brother Jimmy knocked her hand away and she reached to pinch him again. Ashley grinned and poked the preacher in his ribs. Brother Jimmy stared at the stripper's chest. The bulldog gave a low pitched growl. Ashley White moistened her lips while her newest patron eyed her shoulders and waist. The bulldog licked himself again. Redundant foreskin retracted over the canine's glans. Ashley giggled and rolled her eyes.

The black man looked amused as he reached for a pork rind in a brown paper sack. His great white teeth beamed like a trial lawyer's sprawling billboard on the hillside of a busy highway. "Wish I could do that," the dark-skinned patron confessed.

Heavy D looked at his mascot as the bulldog serviced himself again. "Cat Man, that dog would bite you if you tried!" The bartender's belly jiggled again as he reached for a pack of smokes.

"Do you have any more of that twenty-year-old scotch?" Ashley said, looking at Heavy D.

His thick palm twisted a cap off a cold beer. "No, but we have some pretzels that have been around for a while," he said. "Want some?" Heavy D wiped his brow and grinned.

"Hey, Jimmy, why don't you stick around tonight?" the bartender said. "It's Cherry's birthday. The owner paid for a band."

"Definitely," Ashley said as she reached for the preacher's hand. "Eighties cover band."

The owner, Brother Jimmy thought. *Ah, yes. He is her lord and master.*

"I don't know," the preacher said. "I should probably head back home."

"I'm going to freshen up," Ashley said as she tickled Brother Jimmy with a cool hand on the back of his neck. "Don't you want to watch me on stage?" She slithered past the preacher and kissed him on the cheek.

Cat Man sipped a beer at the bar. A short plaster cast covered his left hand and wrist. "Get well soon, nigga," someone had written in plain black letters. It was good for conversation. He enjoyed the attention.

"Cat Man, what in the hell have you done to your hand?" Heavy D asked.

"Well, sah, damn near cut one of my fingers off."

"Aw, you're shittin' me! The whole finger?"

"No, praise the Lord. It was the one next to it!" Puffy lips spread wide to uncover his magenta gums. His big nose expanded to get more air because it was free.

Heavy D grinned. His eyebrows lifted with surprise. The big belly wiggled with laughter. Heavy D was hungry again. The bulldog stood and barked at the black man. "Get'm, Bully! Let's find something to eat."

One of the bouncers walked past the bar. His enormous biceps split the sleeves of his tee shirt. A sullen face carried the expression of a man who could not smile. The black man smirked and looked away. A cigarette dangled from his lips.

Heavy D recalled the black man's last visit to the club.

"Hey, I want to ask you a question," the black man had said.

"Shoot, Cat Man. What do you want, Cat Man? Anything you want. It's all good."

"Well, I was just thinking about Gertrude. You see, uh, Gertrude ain't never been on a honeymoon and we've been married six years. I was gonna ask you . . . see, uh, can you to loan me forty dollars so I can take her on a honeymoon? And I'll sure pay you back."

"What are you going to do with forty dollars, Cat Man?"

"Well, I want to take Gertrude to Nashville for the weekend, so we can have a nice honeymoon."

"Are you really gonna to take her on a honeymoon, Cat Man?"

"Yessah, sure am, sure am. And I'll sure pay you back."

Heavy D loaned Cat Man the money and he left the joint.

The bartender awoke from his daydream. "Haven't seen you in a while, Cat Man. How was your trip?"

"Aw, well, it took us a few days to get over it. But I'm glad you loaned me the money, and I'll sure pay you back."

"Well, did you have a good time in Nashville?" Heavy D spoke to him from across the bar.

"Aw, we had such a good time, sure did, sure did. And I sure appreciate you."

"Did you stay in a nice hotel?"

"Yessah. Sure did, sure did. And I sure appreciate you."

"That's good, Cat Man. Did you eat well?"

"Oh, yessah. Sure did. Ate the best food, sure did, yessah."

"Well, what about Gertrude? Did she have a good time?"

"Uh, well, sah," the black man said. "I got to talking to her and, uh, well, Gertrude had done been to Nashville twice when she was a little girl, so I took her sister, Pamela."

"Ha ha ha ha!" Heavy D shook with laughter.

Cat Man sneered and scanned the room. "Ol' Bully has seen more lips than a nigger dentist," the black man said. The bulldog's droopy jowls spread thin as he yawned and looked away. Cat Man never tipped. It was the running joke among the girls at Babe's. "How do you keep your boat from tipping?" Diamond had whispered in Cherry's ear at the bar late one night when they both were high. "Paint it black," the other stripper replied.

The bulldog growled at the black man as he drank his beer.

"Go get'm, Bully." Heavy D reached for his smokes. "Say Jim, have you heard the Little Johnny joke about the difference between theoretically and actually?"

"No."

"Little Johnny asked his dad the difference between theoretically and actually. And his dad said, 'If you really want to know, go ask your mom and sister if they would sleep with the postman for a million dollars.' So the boy did as he was told. Both women said 'Yes' and he returned to his dad with their answers. And his dad said, 'See, Little Johnny, there you have it: Theoretically we're millionaires, but actually we're living with whores!'"

The bulldog yawned again.

VI

A businessman approached the bar. "The usual," he said without expression and one hand behind his back. The man stood with a serious expression. He brushed his khaki pants, then looked at his watch. A plank of cedar above the counter bent under the weight of various liquors. He had tried every kind and liked them. "Sure thing," Heavy D said. His wide hand reached for a tumbler. He inverted the glass high in the air to see if it was clean. The inscription on the bottom read, "Made in the U.S.A." Heavy D slid the regular patron his drink. Dark amber whiskey looked blameless as it swirled in the stumpy glass. The businessman took a seat by the stage.

Brother Jimmy looked at the selection of liquors. A half-empty jar of corn whiskey stood among the crowded group of spirits. Its white label read: "Shine on Georgia Moon . . . Less than 30 days old."

"Want a drink?" Heavy D said as he faced the preacher. "Glass of corn whiskey? Huh, huh." The best moonshine came from his bearded uncle in Arkansas. The family's whiskey still stood in the corner of the dressing room at Babe's. The frame was fashioned with care, homemade; its wooden legs wobbled with each use. Moonshining requires patience and skill. A hillbilly savors his best work.

"No, thank you," the preacher said as he swirled his straw in the Dixie cup. *Wine is a mocker. Strong drink is raging.* A faithful patron guzzled his beer next to the stage.

"Doobie?" Heavy D smirked as he held a joint.

"No," Brother Jimmy said abruptly. *The body is a temple. Garbage in, garbage out.* A pink flamingo hung from the wall above the bar. This was no place for The Pietà. Redneck yard art was fitting on display. The club was no better than a raunchy trailer park. Brother Jimmy watched as a trio of strippers walked into the club in their street clothes and went immediately to their dressing room. Heavy D looked sternly at one of the girls as she waved and smiled at him shyly. He was their ring leader, or was it the owner, who was seldom there?

"Hey, I'm taking the girls to the casino for late night in a couple of hours," the bartender said. "They're always up for a good time. Won't cost you a dime. It'll be my treat. Wanna come?"

Casino gambling in Mississippi is a grotesque spectacle–bases loaded with retard at bat: four-hundred-pound-plus black and white women riding electric wheelchairs to support their immense gravitational pull, simultaneously gorging on complimentary hot wings and jumbo cocktails of every kind, chain-smoking while receiving supplemental oxygen via nasal cannula. An unseen bell continues its eternal ring to announce that some poor mullet from Wynne, who is far in the hole, just won back a measly twenty-five hundred bucks, holding court over two or three penny slots at once because their arms do reach that far, and funding the whole affair with federal-tax subsidies and big-government giveaways earmarked for the poor, disabled, and disenfranchised.

The pit boss's shit-eating grin makes you gag until he turns and walks away. No need for cold hard cash–coins will do just fine. The Lord always provides. The fattest women spill their sausage-cheese plates and curse a nearby waitress because it must be someone else's fault. And then what do they do? Ask for another, of course. Blame never falls on those plainly responsible.

"No thanks," Brother Jimmy answered with a poker face. His mind turned inward. A single den of iniquity was enough for one day. How honorable are those who stand for something good, refusing to blend in?

"Okay. That's cool. Thought I would ask. That's just the kind of guy I am."

"And I am not," Brother Jimmy replied.

With his coy expression and his arms hanging diffidently by each side, Brother Jimmy's soul withdrew from the wicked scene. His brow held a sense of regret. The fat guy who tended the bar shifted in an uncomfortable pause, sizing up his moral foe, his arch rival in the certain game played by every man. Heavy D was built like a Maytag. Babe's of Memphis was no place for worry.

"Hey, Jimmy. Did Ashley tell you about seeing the lights turned on for the first time at the football stadium in Oxford?"

"No, she didn't," the preacher answered stiffly.

"Sometimes things happen in life that are so crazy you couldn't make them up," Heavy D said.

"What do you mean?" Brother Jimmy's head

tilted slightly as he crossed his arms in front of his chest and reached for his glass of root beer. Heavy D looked for an ashtray.

"Well, before he retired, my old man was lead negotiator for a lighting corporation here in Memphis. He did all the large sales, you see, big commercial sales for the company nationwide, but he worked mainly in the South. Any contract over a million dollars involved him, and he was present at each installation. My father's company bid on the job to put lights in Vaught-Hemingway, and they got the contract. It took thirty-four workers to install the lamps and grid."

Brother Jimmy moved forward to lean on the bar.

"So, they had a meeting at nine o'clock on the night they were going to do the aiming, and he took me along. The university president and entire coaching staff were there, members of the board of regents, too. The whole press box was slammed full, standing room only. Must have been a hundred people there. We even had, um, what do you call it? Hors d'oeuvres." Heavy D took a drag from his cigarette. The preacher's face held a neutral expression.

"Well, the president asked my dad when he was going to turn on the lights and he said, 'Midnight.'

"'Midnight. Great. Can't wait.'

"The atmosphere was electric, buzzing. Not a dry palm there. Everybody was excited. Finally, it came time for the countdown: Ten, nine, eight . . . three, two, one. The engineers threw on the lights. Bam! Boom! Boom! Bam! Pow! And guess what was on the 50-yard line, right on top of the school logo."

"No idea," the preacher said. Heavy D ashed his cigarette.

"There was this girl, looked like a beauty queen spread eagle out there. And there was this guy, one of the football players, the quarterback, was giving it to her . . . Bam! Bam! Bam! Bam! 'Oh! Oh! Yes! Yes! Oh! Oh!' Their moans ricocheted across the stadium and back again. Bam! Bam! 'Oh! Oh!'

"The chief engineer said, 'Quick! We got to kill the lights!'

"But my old man said, 'No. Let him finish.' So I just sat back and watched.

"The chief engineer said, 'What?!' And my father said, 'If you shut those lamps off, they'll never be right. You'll warp everything in them.'

"The university president and head football coach fought over the binoculars. And the football player, the quarterback, never looked up 'til he finished. He just kept going. Bam! Bam! Bam! Bam! 'Oh! Oh! Yes! Yes! Oh! Oh!' Then they stood up, unashamedly. Just stood up, pulled their britches up, and hauled ass, holding hands and laughing all the way.

"The next week that same beauty queen came here looking for work. Something about needing money for school 'cause she was on her own. And her name was Ashley White."

Heavy D took a sip of his beer.

VII

Good music tells a story that no man's tongue can utter. The keyboard player kept perfect time, a drummer led the way. Wooden sticks broke into an eerie solo, stoking a young dancer's fluid bones. The rhythm stirred your feet. It takes a repetitive thump to make girls move. The band cracked off another '80s hit. The sound was crisp and strong. Tall speakers roared loud music 'til the break of dawn. The composition was a perfect beat. A pulse surged in Ashley's heart–it made her want to dance. Darts popped on a colorful board in the far corner of Babe's. Players tossed their sharp points on the board here and there. Glassy eyes aimed for a red bull's eye at chest height in front of a white stone wall. The small circle was safe in the drunken man's line of fire. A well built bouncer surveyed the smoky room. The drummer rolled hard on his snare.

Neon lights brought hot ladies. Every woman fetched a man. Adrenaline rushed in the crowded room when a sexy coed took the stage. She thrived on attention, craved a quick fix. A working man's wallet flopped open with urgent regard. Crumpled dollars flowed. Toned legs spread wide to admit an eager look from the eyes of a bored married man, a convicted felon, the sheltered Baptist preacher who forgot why he had come. Compliance with a Lenten diet did not preclude the devoted priest from perusing a menu. Why should he not have a quick look while he was there? Lust was all around–you accepted it like the shape of your nose or the length of your . . . .

The bouncer sat and watched; he did not get excited. He was numb from years of hackneyed indulgence and too often had seen every girl naked on the lofted stage. Now he was bored. The restless patrons knew who was in control, everyone stayed in line.

She paints her eyes as black as night,
Pulls those shades down tight.

The whole platform was hers. She knew every inch, ushered every perv. There was no turn she could not make, no seductive twitch left unrehearsed. Her bustle was as fluid as a freshly poured draft beer on the corner of Second and Beale. Ashley's perky breasts wiggled cutely as she danced. Her moves were as daring as a wild boar hog.

Lust pooled in the preacher's veins while he watched from his table a few feet from the stage. His heart pumped harder with the lewd act involving two naked girls on the far side of the club, their private parts exhibited shamelessly for desperate men to view. He turned his eyes to Ashley again. His member swelled and throbbed.

A deviant mind works better if rehearsed. She practiced too much. Who needs a choreographer with a name like Ashley White? The club was a forbidden fruit stand on one side of a two-lane county road. A man did not have to rush. There were plenty of melons to go around. Take any you like–they have all been carefully inspected. Bare chests were common as kudzu. They lived at the top of a brass pole center-stage. The air smelled of cocoa butter.

Acrobatics were the chief virtue. There was no safety net at Babe's. To be sure, the clandestine owner did not bother with workman's comp. So what if a clumsy dancer fell off the pole, broke her neck, and never walked again? Another set of fake tits was waiting in the dressing room to take her place. The owner did not care: "Pay the doctor, bitch. No one made you fall." Would an insurance company provide coverage for medical treatment rendered after trauma sustained during willful participation in a potentially hazardous sexual act? Not if they knew about it.

Female forms were in plain view and to a sheltered Baptist preacher looked mighty fine. Frontal nudity spanned the stage. You saw the tan breasts across the smoky room torpedoing off glittered chests like some vital military exercise, the nipples waving here and there as a beautiful woman's body spun on a shiny pole. A clever stripper has more moves than a monkey with a six-foot rope. Ashley's silly smile looked like a chimp's. The painted face barked orders like a veteran drill sergeant demanding money for a stiff drink to silence his lively nerves. A fluorescent sign on the wall read: Coldest Beer, Cheapest Smokes.

She liked being topless. The hard-working dancer spilled her true character without saying a word. Men gaped at hot women walking tall for a buck in Memphis' hottest club. The room was peppered with petite dancing girls. They scavenged here and there, looking intently for cold hard cash. They were insects corrupting the summer garden out back, ubiquitous as pig dung on a busy farm. Ashley's body moved for anyone who needed help getting aroused. Grown men froze with the rigor of week-old road kill. They were dead because of lust. The beer in every hand was cold. Single dollar bills were sprinkled all over the stage. Men emptied their pockets without reserve. The gullible went for broke in front of women who slithered past each other like the reptile that moves on its belly. Insects scattered in an instant when exposed to the bright light of a sunny day, then exploded in a small burst when an indicting conscience got too close.

She keeps a lock of hair in her pocket,
She wears a cross around her neck.

"Father, forgive them," Brother Jimmy mumbled. Desperation was melted on his face. King Solomon spoke to his single trainee: "Give not that which is holy unto dogs, neither cast your pearls before the swine."

Master and man came from the same stock, served the same God. For just how long no one knew, but the great divorce would tell. Ashley's face was as insolent as the soul it covered. She was in full view of the handsome minister's inquisitive gaze. Her naked style was the same as that of all mankind at the start: We enter the world crying for a reason we do not know and displaying our privates as though childbirth were a frantic show-and-tell. Alas, man is born naked, wet and hungry: it only gets worse from there.

The Tri Delta body was perfectly shaped, more than ready for Memphis primetime. She was proud of that tight little ass. Innocence was worse than shame, which was more costly and more boring than regret. Life was on a pole for the world to see. Ashley White belonged on stage in a smoky room packed with encouraging men.

Modesty? the stripper thought. *What's that*?

She was a fast machine;
She kept her motor clean;
She was the best damn woman
that I ever seen.

Ashley descended the glowing steps by the stage and made a line for the preacher's heart.

"How about a lap dance? They're 2-for-1 after midnight." She pointed at her wrist.

"Uhm, I don't think so," Brother Jimmy said. There was timidity in his voice. His small form shuddered. His face was insipid, his manner shy. He looked at his aggressor askance.

The stripper looked at him with purpose. Ashley spoke delicately into the heavy Memphis air and entered the depths of his tender heart. The night was warm with the inviting smell of a sexy young woman who knew how to move. The soft skin of a coed's tan legs would feel good in his hands. Her eyes looked about with casual repose.

"Who'll keep a lookout for people we know?" he asked.

"Here?" Ashley giggled. "In the VIP?" She scoffed at his alarm. "Ha ha! No one, silly!"

"Is it me you like or the idea of me?" he wondered aloud. This he should not have asked. "Am I just as good as any man to drag along for a quick ride, or is there something more?"

"Let's have fun!" She beamed. Her eyes flickered with enthusiasm. Her hands moved longingly over his chest. The two talked as though alone in an ancient garden. Ashley's legs were freshly shaven. Her soft young thighs pressed against his. She belonged on a pom squad.

"I like you," she snickered. Her charm was pure. She was not trashy, just lost. The gospel had not pierced her heart.

Does she have one? he wondered.

"I am an artist," she said with phony self-importance. She did not carry a business card.

A wacky sex act was in her head–the thought was weird.

"Doubtless, that's true," the preacher agreed. But where were her paintings, her busts? Many a starving artist had wandered astray, but never as far as the skid row on a lighted stage, never into the seedy double-life of a lovely coed turned Memphis stripper. A sign over the bar read: Babe's–Oh, yeah, we've got'm!

"I am tortured and complex," Ashley said.

"Indeed, you are," Brother Jimmy agreed.

They moved into a private space. "Not all whores are women, Brother Jimmy," the young stripper said. She pulled her thong to one side in the front, exposing herself as she wiggled her breasts in front of his face.

"Please," the preacher said, "call me Jim." He clasped his hands in front of his waist. She faced him with burning desire. "Really, I insist," he said.

"Anything for you, preacher man," Ashley replied. A hit tune roared overhead.

"I may be a nude dancer, but I am not a whore." The music boomed around them; a singer belted a popular chorus. The sound was bold and full of feeling. The pitch gathered with vigor in a wink as Ashley's flushed cheeks came into the minister's clear view. He thought of her vulva shaved carefully in a warm tub when no one else was around. Her heart pounded with the rhythm of life emerging with a force no man could tame. She needed a stable friend to count on when times were hard. Someone whistled at another stripper who stepped onto the stage.

"You don't think I'm a whore, do you, preacher man?"

"Don't call me that," he said, "at least not in here." He had no sermon to preach in a bordello. There was no pulpit by the brass pole at Babe's. He looked at the big-lipped patron who watched them from his nest by the stage.

"Okay, but you don't, do you? I wasn't always this way," Ashley said. Her decline did not begin at Babe's. It was merely perfected there. At last, the silhouette of her destruction took full shape–an exhausting sculpture touched by a master artist's hand, then hurled into Memphis primetime for every curious eye to see.

VIII

She played the horrible night again in her mind–alone in the sprawling Oxford condo owned by a wealthy man. His wife's fancy paintings adorned the cream colored walls–her handsome fiancé would surely follow in his father's steps.

"Hey, Dad," Kevin said. "Ashley was supposed to meet me here, but she's running late and wants to finish getting ready upstairs. Just tell her I'm at the Square, okay?"

"Will do," his father said.

Wealth had an encompassing aroma her soul could not ignore–its effect consumed like an evil curse. Unease weighed forcibly on Ashley's heart as she pulled into the drive. A banker's pay served the family well. Ashley looked the house over with deserving and expectant eyes.

One day Kevin will have his father's easy life. Our children will be spoiled rotten. Her face held an innocent smile. The home's interior reflected its owner's accomplished career as the head of a well known Texas bank. Every room was tastefully finished.

Why is the condo so dark? The Southern air was thick with a foreboding sense of despair. Her mother's nurturing arms seemed a lifetime away.

Should I be here alone? she wondered. After all, he had flirted with her once before, touched her in the small of her back while tailgating in the Grove. The band played "Dixie" by their tent as he grabbed her ass after drinking too much Jack and Coke.

Maybe I should not have gone to the condo at all that night.

Only her fiancé's father was there. His Benz was parked out front.

If only I had carried my purse inside, the one with the can of Mace.

Ashley blamed herself for causing the heinous act. She had knocked gently on the back door of the condo, then opened it calmly and stepped inside.

"Hey, Ashley," her fiancé's father said. "Kevin said he would meet you at the Square. No one else is here. You can finish getting ready upstairs."

The kitchen was quiet and smelled of feta cheese. A few bottles of wine stood uncorked on the island by a silver watch. A framed picture of Kevin on the granite counter eased her mind a bit. He stood next to his younger sister on a white sand beach. The crest of a cool gulf wave froze in the background. Two sea gulls were caught with their wings open in the distance a couple of hundred yards from the peaceful shore. Her mind teemed with the blissful pretense of a long sunset as she sat by the only man she had ever loved. Ashley thought of the soft white sand. She had never been kissed on a beach.

"Oh, that's okay," Ashley said with conspicuous alarm. "I can just . . . ."

He cornered her with a practiced grin. A ceiling fan whirled overhead. His cheeks were flushed with the gaiety of expensive gin. His breath smelled like a citrus fruit. Long thin fingers were sticky from the last cocktail he poured.

"Looks like it's just you and me, honey."

The man held her hair in the back so tight she could not move, then ground himself against her and made a fist with one of his hands. He tugged at her arm and pulled her close, whispering something despicable in her ear. His stare was decided and sure. Light flickered off the chandelier as he groped her, then jerked on the blue cotton blouse, ripping it to expose the shapely chest that was covered snugly by her favorite bra.

"Please," Ashley said in a soft voice.

He was aroused more by the shape of her inviting breasts. She wished her blouse was not so revealing.

"You wore this for me, didn't you?"

A few drops of sweat oozed from under her chin as the terrifying moments drew on.

"Is this what you came here for?"

There was no thought, only impulse–she slapped him hard across the face. The sound echoed down the hall.

His hand tremored wildly as he reached for the knife. Slowly, without expression, he released her bra in the back. Its bright color strengthened his cause. He tossed the knife across the room. Ashley shrieked when the thick handle hit the floor. He steadied his feet, then reached for a switch on the wall behind her. She screamed as the light dimmed.

He jerked her skirt down in an instant and forced himself inside, moving and thrusting without looking at her, then closed his eyes, mumbling about how good she felt. His breaths became deeper and louder. She felt them on her neck as she tried to get away. But he was too strong. He gripped her hair snugly in the back with one hand as she squirmed.

"No! Let me go!" He was rougher the harder she fought, grinning at the thought of her being afraid. She screamed again as he flung her to the floor and thrust his penis in her mouth. She bit him hard with her eyes closed to block his menacing stare. He hit her twice in the face, then choked her until she bit him again. She screamed and he banged her head against the floor, then threw her onto a shiny leather couch and violated her again, moving rougher and faster than before. There seemed to be no end to the rape. He was on top of her and she could not move. His brow wrinkled madly as he gripped her hair with both hands again and braced for carnal delight. The smell of her hair was on his hands. Her face was smeared with blood. His nature was a force she could not tame. He went on without saying an intelligible word until he finished with an icy grin.

"You think you are a princess, don't you?"

It was true. Her father told her as much. "Hey, princess," her father said while shutting the bedroom door. "How's daddy's little girl?"

"Fine."

"You know I love you," he would say.

"I love you, too, Daddy."

She relived the molestations night after night in her head, the interminable sound of her father entering the room after her mother fell asleep.

"Why don't you show Daddy how much you love him?"

Her mother never knew. No one did.

"I love you, princess," he would say.

"I love you, too, Daddy."

Her mind reawakened to the rapist's threatening words: "You are to tell no one about this, not a word. Do you understand?" She sobbed as his warm semen ran down her chest. "Besides, no one would believe you. I'm president of the largest bank in Dallas, you know." Tears streamed down her innocent cheeks as his warning continued intensely. "If you talk, I will kill you." His threat pounded deep inside her delicate chest.

Her soul cowered. "I won't tell."

A few drops of blood fell from between her legs and landed on the hardwood floor. Her lips quivered from the shock she had just endured. Ashley's life was changed forever.

"You are no different than that dead faggot father of yours," the banker said as he bent over to sop up the blood with her blouse.

"What . . . are . . . you . . . talking about?" She could barely talk.

"Oh, yeah," the man said, his speech slurred. He stood bare-chested by the sink in the kitchen. "Why do you think we kicked him out of the fraternity? Ha! That motherfucker would fuck anything, but his sick preference always had two balls and a stick. That's why we nicknamed him Packer. I wanted to out him in college, but our chapter prez said no."

The days that followed were a blur. Her friends comforted her with pills. They brought the good stuff that made her sleep. She was numb with the horror of a virgin's unwilling sex. How could she let go of the pain she had kept bottled up so long? And what about her promise to Kevin? Their engagement had been going well. She had not dropped her magnolia–it was stolen, taken by force, ripped from the moist slit between her legs where only an evil man had been.

You never forget your first time. Like the palpably racist designations "White" or "Colored" over the entrance to a restroom from a by-gone era, the giving of one's virginity is something we can never take back. Regret is a wasted effort: Feel sorry all you want for the loss of your precious flower–innocence is not coming back. What is done is done and always will be. The worst of all possible nightmares had sadly come true. Now the future was hers to face and she would make of it whatever she pleased.

IX

Ashley emerged from her trance. "I really need the money, now that I'm on my own." She giggled and faced him directly, her head tilted to one side. "Got to have something to repent for next Sunday, right, preacher man?" The rock music roared overhead.

"Well, I . . . ," he sputtered.

"I think someone's ready for a lap dance," she said. The stripper's face was young and smooth. She held his heart in the soft space between her legs.

"Come on!" she exclaimed.

Brother Jimmy shifted slightly in his chair and looked away. *You shall not surely die.*

She was every man's most guilty pleasure. The band played on in a smoke-filled room.

Cause the walls started shaking,
The earth was quaking;
My mind was aching,
And we were making it and you
Shook me all night long.

She was the Devil playing games with his gospel and schooling him in the same. Her favorite past-time involved too many men. His game, her rules–it was no use, could never work. They were just too different. A stripper and preacher–what would other people say?

Was Brother Jimmy willing to accept as fact the requisite magic implicit in authentic belief? Could he live like that for the rest of his life? And, moreover, did he want to?

"I should leave now," the preacher said. The confession was in keeping with his most earnest belief. This was the real Brother Jimmy. Are not all smart statements succinctly put?

"I'll make you feel young again," the stripper said. This time she did not lie.

"I think you just did," he said. Brother Jimmy stared at her face and lips.

"Promise?" Ashley said. She touched him

on the cheek. The preacher nodded and looked away.

"Swear on a stack of Bibles?" She caressed him below the belt. His tongue tasted blasphemy when she kissed his lips. He felt the warmth of its flame and moved closer to her nebulous soul.

"Ready to watch my pole control?" she asked. "Burn, baby, burn," she said with succulent lips while caressing the back of his neck.

Faith, he thought as her command registered in his head, *what's the point*? Soul, be damned. This was his life. The greatest feeling in the world would be worth a lifetime of heartache. He lusted for her feminine part, wanting to be inside.

With determined eyes tracking her prey, the tension surged as they kissed in the VIP.

"Ready to hold me close in the dark?" She spun her body like a small child's favorite toy.

"No," he said.

"Not until you see me completely naked, huh?" She smiled at him intensely, eager to please his soul.

His angel was not a centerfold. He did not love her rock 'n roll. Heaven was not a place on Earth or inside a sexy young woman's twisted head. Conscience was a refuge, not a liability. His most heinous sin was not a delight. Clean living implied security. The humble reverend wanted nothing to do with Babylon. He surveyed her smile with care.

"As a man soweth, so shall he reap."

"Ready for a good time?" Ashley's straddle was as wide as her immodest smile. The virgin had not gone looking for sex in the lavish den of an Oxford condo on that fateful autumn night before the homecoming game versus LSU. It was forced on her by her fiancé's rich dad. Virgins were rare beyond the ninth grade in the boring town that she still called home, but she was waiting for the right man.

Now Ashley White knew every trick. Her soft, young legs would feel good in his double bed. Beauty was her closest friend–she would never be alone. Life's lessons of love and heartache surprise innocent souls more than luck. Cool dice move easily in a gorgeous woman's supple hands when the time is right.

"Do you want me in your bed?" She bounced to and fro on his lap, rubbing her crotch alternately on both of his knees in the privacy of their corner slot. "Oh, yeah," she whispered. Every poor chap was the suckling kind. It was indulgence that she relished most. "Are you gonna fuck me, preacher?" She moaned lustfully in a low voice by his ear, then kissed him on the cheek.

So she really was a despicable whore. She killed for survival and for sport. Perfume lingered like venom in her prey. The passing smell was for a purpose and a good one, too. She made good money giving men their fill of love, of lust, of want for her soft hands, seductive lips, and the momentary glance at her perfect breasts. She gave them a feeling that escaped them at home both night and day. That was why they came. The preacher was many miles from home, from church. Prudence was in a simple prayer, a hard wooden pew–far from a dimly lit club that was littered with naked whores and perverted sex on a lofted stage.

"I haven't seen you in the congregation in a while," Brother Jimmy said with a slavish grin. His mind rushed with the expectation of the pleasure he needed most. "How have you been?" The thrill of Memphis was branded on his eager face.

"Oh, fine," she said. "I've been going to this Pentecostal church in Ecru, The God Almighty Tabernacle. It's a Full Gospel church."

"The one on Highway 6?" He reached for her hand.

"Yes, it's the redneck's Holy of Holies. They have snakes and spiders and all kinds of spiritual things that are great for kids." She snickered again.

All strippers used to be somebody's little girl.

"I want a baby," the young woman said. She had never seen swaddling clothes, a live birth. "The world could use another me," Ashley said. She had a look of conviction on her face.

"Say, is it hot in here or do you have this effect on all girls who would like to feel your bare chest on theirs when the lights go out?" She took his hand in hers and licked it gently.

The maestro spun another hit tune while the eighties cover band broke for ten.

Living easy, lovin' free,
Season ticket for a one way ride;
Asking nothing, leave me be,
Taken everything in my stride.

Don't need reason, don't need rhyme;
Ain't nothin' I'd rather do.
Going down, by the time,
My friends are gonna be there too;
I'm on the highway to Hell.

"Talk to me," she commanded. Her cold-blooded eyes pierced his face. He hugged her innocently. She was bitterly determined to break him. Her strategy was simple: Feel him until he felt her back, then ride him as long as she could. She would bite him and not let go.

Moving shadows in top form were something he missed during the pitch black of midnight when he was in school. He was never Mr. Football, had not escorted the homecoming queen. There was another life out there. He had a lot to make up for. Ashley could help in this belated endeavor, and she wanted to do just that. She bounced up and down on his lap, then slowly licked his ear.

This can't be happening. His eyes were planted firmly on her chest. He froze with another glimpse at her perfect face. Ashley White was a sexual treasure no man could resist.

"Don't you just love Babe's?" Some questions imply their answers. "I do," she said with a patented grin. "Mama always said I belonged on stage." Her gape penetrated his flimsy soul.

It was true. Her mother told her someday she would be a star, take a lead role. The Tri Delt was at home in the spotlight, felt at ease on a shiny pole in the nude. Folks drove their cars from miles around to stare while she undressed long after the sun went down on a hot summer night. She was proud to be naked for all to see, and trusting as a newborn babe. A stripper spun faster and faster on the parquet stage.

No stop signs, speed limit;
Nobody's gonna slow me down;
Like a wheel, gonna spin it,
Nobody's gonna mess me round;

Hey Satan, paid my dues,
Playing in a rocking band;
Hey momma, look at me,
I'm on my way to the promised land;
I'm on the highway to Hell.

Whores imagine every man's member. Her costume was delicate and lean. She petted herself through the thin silk wrap-around, making her thong panties wet, then raised a limp satin garment with dainty fingers that never knew love, only lust. Purple sequins glistened under black light. The big game was about to begin: sex was like football–kickoff was on every man's mind, even–no, *especially*–if he was a man of the cloth. There were any number of formations and trick plays. Many were the ways for skilled players to score: on the ground, in the air, during or after a long, exhausting drive. Ashley's polished step gave the home team a distinct advantage.

He's all mine now, the young stripper thought. The human male was like a piece of wood, forgiving most of the time. Start with any old stick and work with it a while–if it does not turn out just right, chunk it in the fire; it will still burn. She drew her thong to one side in the front and put his hand on one of her hips. Wickedness was in an innocent touch. The love that was prosaic still was–but was now also profane.

"I want to suck you dry." She handled his member gently, as though lighting a candle to unleash a fresh scent.

Brother Jimmy pondered his dilemma on the couch. King David did not say no, and he quarterbacked the ancient Jews. Bathsheba was head cheerleader. That ancient whore bent over like a center before the first snap: waiting to move on one man's command initiated by hands exploring wherever they liked and teasing her moist clit before throwing a long touchdown pass. The extra point was another dirty trick. Hormones were not passed out at Brother Jimmy's request. Testosterone was not his idea. He would risk everything he knew and was, and everything he was born to be. Never mind his faithful sheep; they would find another shepherd whose staff was stronger and tamer than his. The head deacon would chair the search.

"Who are you going to satisfy with that little thing?" she asked with a mocking grin.

"Me," he said, not thinking. Ashley giggled mildly.

What would a little fondle hurt? *Just a stroke or two*, he thought. *Then she will stop.* He considered the possibility in his sober head. "You will not surely die," the serpent had said in Genesis. The preacher recoiled with shame. There was nothing new under the sun.

Her nipples quivered with her body's most basic need. She pressed her chest against him gently. "Fuck me, Brother Jimmy," she said. Ashley's chest trapped him inside.

"But what if . . . ?"

"Shhh! Here? Not a chance." She lied in a plotting voice. Her proposition was arrant and plain. The stripper was harsh and untrue. Anything could happen. Rules did not exist at Babe's of Memphis.

Beloved, a whore is capable of every sin.

"And if you conceive?"

"Then it's His will, right?" Ashley said with an arrogant grin.

Brother Jimmy did not object. *It is easier to ask for forgiveness than permission*, he thought. The preacher was clay in the hands of a cheap potter and her name was Ashley White. The show went on as another young stripper's painted face smiled for the cheering crowd. She was made up like a ludicrous clown at a low budget county fair. His conscience told him to leave. Swiftly, and with a loud smack, the door closed behind him. Heavy D slid another patron his foamy beer. A new song began inside.

Loose pebbles crunched underneath his feet in front of the club. The door creaked as he opened it. Heavy raindrops popped on the windshield. He gripped the wheel until his knuckles turned white. The parson was alone somewhere in Memphis. A full moon hung over Graceland. Brother Jimmy's heart beat slowly as put his truck in gear.

The thrill was gone, but he sought consolation and looked to the only source of his strength at church.

PART THREE

PURPLE CHURCH

I

It is a scene repeated often in the under-privileged rural South. The practice never gets old. On Sunday mornings, families eat hearty breakfasts together and ready themselves for a meeting with God. Church façades are like a secretly repentant parishioner's face, covering what is ugly and yet unseen by anyone save the Almighty. Massive Roman columns are admirable and imposing. They frame expensive renderings of the Gentle Jesus in stained glass shipped in a cushioned cargo box from abroad. The colorful windows herald The Great White Throne Judgment promised on a dusty scroll from long ago. Their simple message is critical for all to hear: "Trust in Jesus or receive your sentence now," they effectively imply. The gospel is clear in its eternal reward: *Christ welcomes all who welcome him.*

How does a poor Southern town afford such décor? With manna from Heaven, of course. The weekly offering is served on a padded plate.

"For with God all things are possible," the self-righteous deacon is proud to say. Faithful tithing is a matter of religious priority. You give because you are commanded–God says so. No need to sacrifice a helpless, struggling lamb. Christ's charitable mandate is more flaccid than that. The meek rejoice because the vital action is passive and covert. Flop open your wallet each week–the church will take what you can give. The harvest truly is plentiful. Good Christians believe as they are told.

They come from far and wide to confess sins of every kind, meeting in unflattering sanctuaries where a stuffy minister's sermon reminds hearers of hellfire and brimstone that await those who blaspheme the Word. Sleepy Christians come to life when the Spirit moves. Christ's wounded hand nudges them all. The preacher's yell falls on anyone with ears that are willing to listen, pricking every heart stained by shameful sins committed in haste during a drunken stupor on Friday night.

Deacons nod stoic approval when a visiting reverend damns the bottle, only to take a much-needed drink when his mood mellows late in the day. Dry counties in the Deep South exist only in a teetotaler's puritanical mind as he wages personal jihad against the bottle and the can. "What is the difference between a Baptist and a Methodist?" a favorite Protestant joke begins. The Methodist says "Hello" in the liquor store.

Church pews are crafted from hallowed cherry wood so hard it must be petrified. Chandeliers are mature and lackluster. Their light is dim but holy. Babies, hardly strong enough to be released from the hospital, but too fragile to be rocked in an antique nursery crib apart from their mothers, squall whenever the Spirit moves. The faithful endure lengthy prayers hurried along by fidgety congregants who bark frequent amens to conceal stomach growls amidst a balding deacon's exhaustive prayer. Better to speak up and be heard.

Dinner on the grounds is waiting downstairs for Christians to stuff themselves with fried chicken, casseroles, and scrumptious desserts of every kind. Next Sunday repeats the whole fraught, Spirit-driven cycle all over again. The Protestant sect values repetition as much as its chronic arch rival. A fruitful service needs a blessed twin involving those who yearn for more worship, love, and praise. Evening Service begins promptly at six o'clock. Another offering will be taken then. *Date et dabitur vobis*. Beloved, give again as the Spirit leads.

Across the tracks, a mass of black folk bellows a great Negro spiritual–the ardent expression borne of steadfast belief. An entire community vows to serve with care. The robed choir sways to and fro on its rickety loft like a weighty ship on an ocean topped with a cleansing foam. A wide-based mammy smiles with utter glee. Her solo is heard outdoors:

Oh happy day (oh happy day)
Oh happy day (oh happy day)
When Jesus washed (when Jesus washed)
When Jesus washed (when Jesus washed)
Jesus washed (when Jesus washed)
Washed my sins away (oh happy day)
Oh happy day (oh happy day)

II

He sat in his lair and rehearsed a scripture lesson heard from the cradle. Conscience was in his heart. He was numb with intoxicating guilt. It flowed as strong drink through his veins. The poison left him weak. His pulse slowed as he cried; a pastor has burdens, too. Life was nothing if lacking in ethic. He could not forget what his eyes witnessed the night before, what his mind thought it would never see. Sorrow was in his flesh, his bones. Brother Jimmy's mouth was dry. His throat was tight with worry.

How can I preach like this? Who could speak to the growing crowd instead of me?

He had not eaten a proper meal in days: a wedding, a birth, the tragic death of an important tither made him neglect his body's most primal want. A focused pastor makes time for a filling meal to refresh his penitent heart. The lost did not quickly become so–let them wonder at will. The dead man in the casket could wait. It was the fretting souls gathered around the corpse who made him eat too fast whenever he had a chance. Could he still baptize repentant hearts or administer the Lord's Supper on an empty stomach in the name of the Father, Son, and Holy Ghost?

He clasped his hands together, then placed them under his chin. *Judge Peters is out of town,* he thought. The preacher's heart sank with doubt. Magic was a mandate implicit in belief. Christ was no different from the soothsayers he condemned. The significance of his resurrection escaped unenlightened souls. The divine secret remained covert, like conviction hovering over the humbled sinner's mortal sin. He needed time to think–of life and death, of his once fervent belief and present doubt. He had much to reconcile were he to continue as a man of faith. The office was silent, except for the quiet cadence of the pendulum inside a grandfather clock.

The preacher folded his hands like a praying mantis; he placed bony elbows on the desk. Had Jimmy Russell propagated a laughable myth? Did he believe in an utter lie? Had he staked his claim to an eternal reward on the basis of what others wrote or said? His parents brought him up in the church, but had never seen the risen Christ. Their intentions were pure and sincere, but so were the Buddha's introspective words.

The adulterous memory of a lighted stage shook his heart from the trusty anchor it had known. Now the preacher was left to wonder what he earnestly believed. Could the tarnished soul of a backslidden preacher be cleansed with the spilled blood of an ancient Jew? Was the gospel the biggest hoax ever foisted on the impressionable heart of mortal man or an inexplicable yet irrefutable historical fact to be acted upon by every soul in the human race? Was Christ resurrected or not?

The Faith's best missionary once persecuted those he later befriended. That was the real thorn in his hypocritical Gentile side. Queue the Apostle Paul:

"And if Christ be not raised, your faith is vain; ye are yet in your sins."

Uncertainty clouded his mind. The resurrection was a question of written history. Its eternal conclusion was either the most notable event reported by ancient man or the most awful, vicious hoax infused into the heart of a spiritless man. Brother Jimmy was nothing if not naïve. The gospel truth weighed heavy on his heart. The preacher's eyes rolled back in his head as his stomach churned with doubt. His chest throbbed with unease.

Jesus of Nazareth was a young Jewish carpenter and prophet who claimed to be the Son of God long prophesied in ancient Scripture. He was sold for thirty pieces of silver by one of His disciples who a few hours later hung from a rope. He was arrested for disrupting the religious peace, judged a political and civil criminal, and then crucified on a Roman cross. His dead body was buried in the tomb of a wealthy man who showed Him pity. Three days later some women who went to anoint His body in the tomb found it missing and informed the chosen few. His victory came after a bloody fight won by the hand of Almighty God.

In the weeks that followed, a rag-tag group of disciples professed that God raised Him from the dead. He appeared to them many times before levitating to be with His Father in Heaven's matchless glory. With that simple message, Christianity spread throughout the Roman Empire and exerted tremendous influence throughout a sinful world. Living witnesses propagated the good news at the risk of life itself. New Testament recordings of the resurrection were made known during the time of those who bore witness to the risen Christ. They saw the crucified Jesus alive again. He lived and breathed as they did. If it was not true, why say otherwise?

The writers of the four Gospels either had themselves been witnesses or else were relating the accounts of eyewitnesses to the actual events. In advocating their case for the gospel, a word that meant good news, the apostles appealed, even when confronting severe opposition, to common knowledge concerning the facts of the resurrection and countless miracles that happened before. Beloved, the Lord died and rose again.

Brother Jimmy looked at a replica of Caravaggio's famous painting that hung on his office wall. Framed by an onyx border, The Calling of Saint Matthew demanded his sober attention. For a moment, no one moved. Every action ceased. Ancient men froze in the holy shadow of God the Son. Levi rose promptly in the presence of associates at his money-lending table to assume a different role and name. The gloom of an idle Tuesday was instantly swept away through the canvassed window. The meeting was indoors, inside an unsuspecting tax collector's cheating heart. Christ came to him. The Lord met His subject where he was. Two very different worlds collided and with a mighty force. The true light of God Himself penetrated the dark corner of the tax collector's scheming mind. Christ's omnipotence shook an empty soul and turned the mundane afternoon into a memorable event that centuries later moved the baroque painter's delicate brush, leaving a masterpiece for the world to enjoy.

Brother Jimmy was weak from shame. The sin of a lustful act was upon him. His member was limp from an action that was fresh on his mind. Sexual frustration had brought him low. Life's fragility moved in his brittle soul.

Is there anyone to whom I can turn? he wondered as he sat alone at his office desk.

He looked at the famous painting again.

Jesus shot his disciple with focused light from above while the others sat in darkness. His immortal gesture required no thought at all, yet its strength could not be ignored. The Lord called his disciples to a different path. Brother Jimmy closed his eyes. The preacher's own calling seemed a lifetime away, his commission sublime and stale. Once he walked on holy ground. Now holiness was gone like an ill wind that left him buried deep in the drunkenness of mortal sin.

III

Sunday school started on time. Church bells rang out as the stoic rebel soldier stood proud at the heart of the orderly Court Square. The magnolias were in full bloom. Tardy parishioners sneaked into back rows like children playing a quiet game of cat and mouse. The smallest Christians play many a petty game. Principle, like punctuality, is an in-born trait–either you arrive on time or not.

Brother Jimmy peered out the window from his cozy office. He watched his parishioners trickle in by twos into the vestibule as an eager deacon greeted member and guest. His was a lawyer's able smile, welcoming the lost in want of vision and the hungry in need of succor. He was like Noah, warning of what would come next and ready to move indoors at the first drop of rain.

Congregants made their way up the painted brick steps and into the sanctuary, where the faithful sat ready to learn. Mr. White held open the door for Dr. Rayburn and his wrinkled wife, whose thin lips grinned like a jackass. Contentment is the default emotion of the fortunate few who have not seen the repugnant places in a fallen world. The couple nodded easily to the old man, who prayed silently for the woman's soul.

Organ pipes blew the prelude; an old woman mouthed the chorus as she practiced her notes. The organist looked like a prim Quaker with her grey hair brought back in a bun. You saw her and remembered American Gothic. The painter fancied her by a small cottage in the tidy Midwest. A farmer husband stood near his prim wife. The way to keep sane and lead a meaningful life was to ignore popular culture as much as possible. The prudish life was simple and best. But even a stuffy Baptist needs the occasional thrill.

Brother Jimmy leaned back in his worn office chair. The resurrection was sharp on his mind. He cringed with an involuntary pause at the most miraculous biblical account. Could he still trust what he read from the Holy Book? His mind raced to an improbable turn. What authentic evidence bridged the gap between his painful doubt and unwavering confidence from an earlier time? New Testament witnesses were aware of the fatal consequences administered by Roman guards for telling a crucial lie.

An extremely large rock was rolled against the entrance of Arimathea's ancient tomb. The great stone was not pushed away by mortal man. Something bigger and better was there. No Roman soldier would risk his neck for a lying Jew. He affixed the seal and stood erect to emit the wrath of Tiberius Caesar's clearest law. But the tomb was empty in spite of his show. The Roman guard was nowhere to be found. He ran from soft white clothes while they folded in on themselves, as the Earth shook with power from a Heavenly throne. Grace fell as the frightened guard covered his head before fleeing like a scalded dog. Christ tore through the powerful bond of a Roman seal, and now the primitive cave was empty. The vacant tomb was a matter of history too notorious to be ignored. If His body were still dead, why not parade it through the streets of Jerusalem and prove it so to embarrass the growing number of cheering peasants and make a spectacle out of the riotous, blaspheming Jews?

Christians believe Jesus was resurrected in time and space by the supernatural power of the only living God. The preacher recounted what he professed: "The Lord is greater than every sin." But did Brother Jimmy still believe? *The difficulties of belief may be great, but the problems inherent in unbelief present an even greater question of faith.*

Was The New Testament reliable at all? Was the dead Christ laid in another tomb? Did Mary and Mary, who reported the missing Christ, enter the wrong sepulcher, which happened to be empty, and then spread their findings aloud like ignorant women prone to gossip sometimes do? If so, then the men who verified their claim must also have mistakenly visited the wrong tomb as well. If the Roman guard were not displaced by an earthquake as the *Holy Bible* plainly says, then why did Jewish authorities not produce the dead body and quell every boisterous claim to the contrary?

He thought of the empty tomb and Christian martyrs who despite horrendous physical harm managed to die with their spirits in utter peace. As a reward for their unshakable faith, early Christians were tortured, beaten, stoned, thrown to the lions, or crucified upside down. They sacrificed life itself as the ultimate proof of their utter confidence in the truth of the gospel message. For centuries many of the world's distinguished philosophers assaulted Christianity as irrational, superstitious, and absurd. Many ignored the central issue of Christ's resurrection. Others explained it away through various concocted theories.

But the historical evidence he could not discount. He could not explain or refute the empty tomb. The great stone was not rolled away to permit the Lord's exit, but to give curious witnesses a tangible reason to believe. Christ's followers said he was alive again. His appearance served as infallible proof. The Supper at Emmaus documented one of the alleged accounts. The painting hung on his bedroom wall. A basket of food teetered on the table's edge. *I am teetering as well.* The risen Christ vanished out of sight. *Jesus has left me, too.*

Had the disciples seen an illusion of the risen Christ who fed at the same wooden table as them at Emmaus? Would Brother Jimmy accept the gospel on blind faith as a crafty supernatural trick, or perish with the rest of mankind for being honest about his reasonable doubt?

He thought of Doubting Thomas who dared to specify his unbelief. Then, reaching his hand into the giant piercing on Christ's glorified flesh, he believed what his brethren had said with cheer: "Blessed are those who have not seen and yet have believed."

"Not really," Brother Jimmy said aloud. "It would be better to touch Him."

Faith was the embodiment of cowardly despair, a simple act that perpetuated and enlivened the feeble heart. Brother Jimmy's chest trembled with guilt. His conscience was impugned by his memory of the stripper's enchanting smile. He saw Ashley White again in his dreams and felt her while he slept. Would he feel her smooth legs rub against his once more as they did in the heart of Memphis' hottest club?

Perhaps the match was ordained in Heaven. Brother Jimmy deserved a young and beautiful woman's exciting touch. He earned it through the ascetic life he had lived since his wife's untimely death. His spirit was selfless. Someday he could love her, save her, perhaps even take her in. Their time was coming as soon as she lent her charm and took him by the hand–kissed him, held him–as soon as he gave his lonely heart a needed chance while the strobe lights whirled across his face.

IV

"Father, if it be thy will, take this yoke from me," Brother Jimmy prayed, clasping his hands tightly together as he approached the pulpit. His mind went back to the spacious room on the wrong side of town, to the smoky bar where a sometime coed winked and crossed her legs. No hint of contrition was on his face. He thought of the stripper's bare body moving in the spotlight of a Memphis stage, the wondrous mounds of female flesh emanating from her coed chest, poking out and edging closer, closer to grip his soul and pull him in, the young nipples eyeing his every move, tracking his most private dream, making him flinch with utter surprise and wiggling in jest whenever he did.

The pews were filled with sinners and saints. He preached his sermon as though nothing was wrong.

V

Brother Jimmy sped past a gravel drive on the two-lane road leading north to Memphis. The farms near Ecru renewed his interest in a simpler time and forgotten place. A marquee sign in front of a little church read *God Almighty Tabernacle, Revival Week August 8–12.* A single-wide trailer was parked out back. The widowed church pastor lived there alone. Brother Jimmy helped bury his friend's devoted wife. He did not forget her apostolic slant.

The Pentecostal sect is a curious group: self-effacing pale women who never look in a mirror, long grey hair that does not get cut, denim skirts reaching to cankles, acceptance of smelly armpits and abhorrence of makeup. Emotional rage is, in fact, their collective default. The pew-jumper's fervent dedication to the God he has felt but never seen gives the ignorant visitor a reason to shout: "Yea for God! Jesus is King!" The more liberal variety drink Coke with their Lord's Day lunch.

"Pentecostal"–the word says it all.

After a wrong turn he was on the freeway and entering unfamiliar ground. He took the exit ramp to Poplar and was soon facing west. Just beyond the overpass, he saw a parked hearse under a portico. Solid chrome wheels shone back at a turning car's lone headlight across the street. A small bird saw its reflection in one of the wheels and flew away, taking refuge in a nearby shrub. A siren wailed on a dead-end street close by. Brother Jimmy drove past a large cemetery, a funeral home, and the furniture store that bore its owner's Jewish name. His stomach growled with discontent. Hunger is one of life's recurring pains.

He turned into the parking lot of a quaint café. The yellow brick building had the look of a well-kept home on a prosperous farm in Eads. The owner was a self-made man. A draft notice cut short his promising career in the major leagues. Two hits of shrapnel nearly cost him his innocent life, but still he was not bitter. His heart was strong, his mind was sure. Mike Richmond was born to lead.

"Welcome to Blue Plate Café," the waitress said with a natural smile. "What'll you have this evening?"

Brother Jimmy's gut rumbled. He scanned the menu with nervous eyes. "Chicken and dumplings," he said.

"Okay." The waitress scribbled happily on her spiral bound pad. "And to drink?"

"A glass of sweet tea with lemon."

"Coming right up," the waitress said. The preacher placed both hands in his lap. The walls were decorated with original animal paintings done by the owner's wife. The scenes were filled with color, the faces were docile and tame. Brother Jimmy imagined a zoo. A bold lion's stare made him weak.

The happy waitress returned with his tea,

then quickly left the room. Another patron nodded from across the room. The man looked stout and gruff; there was an air of steady triumph on his face. His quiet manner implied success.

"Pardon, me," the preacher said. "How do I get to Winchester?"

"Winchester," the man said as he slowly chewed his food, "Well now, that's a major road in town and a long one, too. Where are you trying to go?" he said as he buttered a slice of bread.

"Well, uh . . . ."

The two men were alone in the stylish room.

"Not going to one of those unholy places are you?" The stranger was blessed with intuition. He gave a subtle grin after he sipped his drink. Brother Jimmy was quiet and still. His hands moved back and forth on his lap.

"Better not set foot in the Purple Church," the other patron said. "That place is a stubborn fortress of ill-repute." He spoke plainly while he chewed.

"I beg your pardon." Brother Jimmy appeared confused.

"Ah, yes, the Purple Church: Where dreams are destroyed and hearts are broken." The man reached for his glass of tea. "Sexy little coed took my soul and robbed me blind in there one night last week."

The preacher pressed his lower back against the chair.

"And let me tell you," the man said, "she had the best set of titties I have ever seen."

VI

Bright lights beamed toward a starless sky. The radiant plume over Memphis showed him the easy way. Sin had a sparkle that caught his eye –it burned and consumed like the hottest flame. A horn blew in the distance down a vacant street when he stopped at a traffic light. A black man on a bike peddled by lazily and cursed the heat.

"Memphis, baby, Memphis," the man mumbled to himself, "Makin' easy money pimpin' hoes in style."

Blue lights atop a police car bounced from the rear-view mirror. The preacher's heart raced with surprise, and he held hard to the wheel. In a second, the policeman sped by.

"Whew," he said.

He drove with purpose on a dimly lit street where rundown shanties coalesced like a flooded sewage lagoon, then headed farther west into the wasteland of metro Memphis: an expanding cesspool of pawn shops, payday loan joints, discount tobacco and WIC outlets, used car lots, tattoo parlors, vacated strip malls, convenience stores fitted with dark steel bars, and the offices of well-fed bail-bondsmen eagerly awaiting their next hire. Poverty and vice were cancers, too, as aggressive and persistent as any rapidly fatal malignancy ever was.

He gripped the wheel tighter and continued northwest on Lamar. The traffic stopped him by a package store. A neon sign in the window flickered a familiar logo. He looked to his right and spotted a mangy stray dog hunting for food. He looked to his left and nodded subtly at a homeless vet who sat on a chair with canted wheels, then drove on toward the corner of Mulberry and Huling, past the place where a foolish white man martyred the vocal champion of civil rights and united an entire race for a worthy cause: "Oh happy day (oh happy day)."

On the other side of town, men and women carried on at the close of day. They drove their cars southward along the Big Muddy, cruising to the various bustling sounds played over FM. A few passed toward their familiar destinations with an urgent sense of habitual purpose, but most of them just looked straight ahead with no emotion at all. No feeling of haste or joy moved weary heads at the end of a hectic day. Clothes that were neatly pressed a few hours before now smelled like the work that had just been done. A puffy cloud hung low in the southern sky. The pearly moon looked on as a dark sky hovered close to Graceland, and all over Memphis the muggy air portended rain.

The preacher's soul lay uncovered for him to inspect. His chest was cracked, his heart exposed, beating slower and weaker, pumping feebly yet still enough to keep him alive. He had turned from his Baptist roots to worship the face of a tormented stripper who could not say no. She did not care when her life would end and now neither did he.

The scene at Babe's was no different than the night before. Heavy D was just as fat. A frumpy divorcee spewed more off-color jokes into a microphone on one side of the stage. His manner was cynical and nonchalant.

"How do you get the flies out of your kitchen?" the divorcee asked.

The attentive crowd braced for a laugh.

"Move the bucket of shit into the living room!"

"Is that the best you got?" a heckler yelled.

"Yeah!" another man cried.

There once was a woman named Alice
Who used a dynamite stick as a phallus;
They found her vagina in South Carolina
And the rest of poor Alice in Dallas!

"Ha! Drink up boys!"

"Give us another!" one of the perverts shouted.

"Okay, okay," the divorcee said before taking another gulp of his beer. "What are the three shortest books in the Library of Congress?" The crowd was impatient and tense. "*Harvard Football Heroes*, *Jewish Business Ethics*, and *Africans I Have Yachted With*!"

"Ha! Ha! Ha! Ha!" The patrons howled. "Fuck me naked and burn my clothes!" someone shouted from the corner.

The joker returned to a table by the bar. Putrid breath kept his peers a safe distance away. The smell of stale garlic leaped from each word. He wore a dark undershirt beneath his plaid button-down. The man's armpits were moist with sweat. His face was stoic as he took his first drink of the night. He sipped his beer guiltily–a policeman gets fired for drinking on duty. The man dropped a small silver badge into the front pocket of his faded shirt: Captain, Memphis PD. He spotted a young sergeant on a stool by the bar.

A group of lawyers had a table to themselves. They listened reflexively to a sharply dressed accountant who attempted to entertain them on stage: "The whole world finally dies and an endless line forms at the pearly gates of Heaven. Suddenly, there is a loud roar from the front of the line. Men throw their hats in the air and give each other high-fives. A man in the back yells, 'Why are you cheering?' And someone up front says, 'They're not counting adultery!'"

The lawyers grinned slyly; one of them laughed before sipping his drink. The strippers slithered passed them without hearing a word. A stale-smelling man followed on stage.

"Why do women rub their eyes in the morning?"

"No idea!" a sleazy attorney shouted from the back of the bar.

"Because they don't have any balls to scratch!"

The crowd chuckled as a trio took the stage and sang a raucous tune in iambic pentameter:

I wish that all girls were like bricks in a pile,
And I were a mason I'd lay them in style!
Oh, roll your leg over,
Oh, roll your leg over,
Roll your leg over–
It's better that way!

I wish that all girls were like statues of Venus,
And I were a sculptor with a petrified penis!
Oh, roll your leg over,
Oh, roll your leg over,
Roll your leg over–
It's better that way!

The horny patrons roared with approving

laughter as luscious bodies glided smoothly across the dimly lit stage. Puffs of fresh smoke emerged from a loveseat scorched by lust in the pit of Hell. A strange couple sat on a black vinyl chair. The stripper fit just right in her client's cheating lap. The two knew not each other. Names did not matter. They knew their roles. No one was a victim here, in the den of lustful intrigue. A sign over the bar read: *Tuesday Longnecks 2-for-1*. The light shone as bright as a pervert's hungry stare. A fire chief gawked by the stage. The words on a gallon tip jar read: *Lead us not into temptation, we already know the way.*

I wish that all girls were like blades of grass,
And I were a mower I'd cut me some ass!
I wish that all girls were like bats in a steeple
And I were a bat
There be more bats than there are people!
Oh, roll your leg over,
Oh, roll your leg over,
Roll your leg overrrr . . .
It's better that way!

Life was on the pole, hard-edged and serious. Ashley's curves were present for every paying man to see and touch in a dark corner of the VIP. Stripping was an end to something more. Real talent paid better than honest work. She knew the game and played it well. The careful smile, the tender touch–both belonged to her. She invented the slighting hand, her grip trapped every man. The pole was a playful thing, like her best friend from second grade. Ashley pranced here and there like the proud animal that she was. She smiled like a silly chimp and fell into her client's lap. Her blue eyes were thick with a glassy sheen. The young veins were numb with the steady high of her latest bar that was served by the hand of Heavy D. She laid face down on the stage, pretending to hump the floor, then spun her eyes at the preacher's face.

Brother Jimmy clasped his hands as he sat and watched. His manhood throbbed harder with her undulating moves. The pleasure had escaped him since the onset of his late wife's fatal disease. He leaned back in the chair and thought: *What if the pagans are right*? Cool music whined overhead. *What if there is no God, no Christ*?

Standing on the corner it's easy to see,
forbidden fruit is on every tree.
Oh, you can buy an apple from a snake on a limb.
He's just looking for a sucker that he can take in.

Ashley led him to a couch when a new song played. "How about a dance?" the young stripper said.

"Uhm, I . . . ." His eyes scanned her glittered chest.

"Come on!" Ashley petted his arm and smiled. She was the living and breathing unscrupulous whore he often wailed against.

Brother Jimmy's toes curled with a tension they had never known. Ashley's lips were inviting and smooth. In her busy manner and polished style, she gave the effect of a finished canvas worth the cost of admission required to ascertain her actual worth. She crossed her legs and winked at him.

"Don't you want a house of your own?" he asked. "A yard?"

"Not really," she said in a trance. "Home is where your feet are." The stripper's eyes danced when she spoke. The pastor's pleasure was her only conscious goal. Ashley puckered her lips and blew a cool wind over a breath mint, then flicked her tongue in Brother Jimmy's face like the slithering reptile that she was. His eyes shook at a sight they had never seen. Would he ever truly know her? Could he be so lucky in the biblical sense? She moved closer to his chest and neck. The softest place on Earth dwelled in Ashley's flesh and smelled just as it felt.

She reached for the moist slit he wanted to see, then escorted him to a private suite in the VIP. The stripper sat topless on the black leather couch and toyed with his member, her soft hands working wonders as it moved up and down. She stopped for a moment and lit a scented candle, then touched him and made it count, brought him to life again. Brother Jimmy jolted forward with a half-hearted thrust. Lust welled inside his neck and chest. Passion is the original temptation an honest clergyman fights but cannot tame. He reached for the perfect breasts as they jiggled cutely in their quest to tease and rob.

"We're being bad," Brother Jimmy said.

"Only the good die young," she replied without expression. "That's why I try to be a bitch half the time." The preacher's arms were limp. Ashley opened her mouth to lick his finger, then suck him in, leading him on to the dark and endless journey he was painfully scared to take. Her face beamed with fateful pride when she leaned over to kiss his neck.

"Are you real?" he wondered aloud. This he should not have asked. She listened to him breathe as his shaft inflated in her silky hand. The Memphis air was thick with lust. Ashley grinned, enticing her prey again. Her nipples were hard and mean.

"I'm as real as you are," she said. "Pinch me and I cry. Cut me and I bleed." She reached for the preacher's hand. "And sometimes I bleed, even if I am not pinched," she added coolly. A thin silver cross hung from a necklace in the little cleft between the top of her breasts. She rested her arms on his shoulders while sitting on top of him, enthroned like an ancient heiress who ruled over a wide domain.

"It's tough being a woman." She sighed, then looked away. A new song roared in the club. "At least I rule on the stage at Babe's."

And yet she served every man.

VII

Their action was perfectly legal. She was ready for a sex-filled spasm that would shake every bone, and he was a consenting adult. There was no crime committed here. Intercourse was completely lawful in Tennessee and more important than any sinner's tearful prayer. Enduring participants reported in tip-top form, lest they awake to find the friction left them dry and sore. The sex tales of real life are more entertaining than Hollywood's best love scene. A single-wide trailer rocks back and forth under the weight of a new marriage bed, squeaking until its new slats get broken in. A fat Bubba has a libido, too.

Brother Jimmy was sweaty and tense. His suppression of lustful desire fueled a fire in his heart that made its red flames turn hotter as his soul prepared to burn. Ashley was sexier than the moment before. They were like David and Bathsheba. The preacher was outspoken and cheered for God, his mistress was captain of the pom squad. The Spirit left him in haste.

"There is nothing new under the sun."

They were all alone in the VIP. A few moments passed while they spoke. The light was dim. Her placid strokes made more potent juices flow. His member was as hard as the brass pole on which the naked dancer swung at center stage. They went further still.

She milked him with both hands as he looked away and thought, *Is this what living was meant to be*? The preacher felt good again–in the presence of Heaven or Hell he could not say.

A tight young body is every man's most earnest desire. Ashley's horny body begged for more. She spoke her commands without saying a word.

If it feels good, do it, he thought.

She straddled him and took control. With her head leaned back and her eyes closed, she pushed him inside her a tiny bit at first, then all the way. His member was long and she took every inch. A man's stamina mattered most. How long could a pastor go?

She referred to her designer watch. *Bet this won't take long,* she thought inside her conniving head. She glanced at him with possessing intent. Only time would tell. She was right–her dead eyes gripped him like the blank stare of an untamed animal playing for keeps.

Dancing was a time when life reached a sort of pinnacle, a highlight to be remembered until the next show tune played. She was no debutante–that required some measure of decency. She could not afford Walt Disney. Rarely has a stripper seen The Happiest Place on Earth. Ashley White could only imagine such a perfect place. Coitus was a rural county fair that came and went in the blink of a sexy coed's eye. Rusty metal rides were the closest thing to entertainment in the small town where she was raised. They creaked louder with every slow and repetitive turn. His erection was the Ferris wheel for her to play on, and he would pay her cash to ride. What else was there to do, save bounce up and down like a rubber ball, rolling and ricocheting from the spinning top to the merry-go-round that some toothless carnie neglected to oil?

With her painted face and glittered chest, she demanded a second look from the man with a boyish grin.

"I want us to fuck 'til the cows come home." She rode him hard and mean. A final hump of her toned hips and he let go inside her moist little slit. She touched him and the deed was done. The preacher licked his lips and moved to kiss her again. He finished in a flash of sheer carnal delight.

"Here, take this." Brother Jimmy handed her a crisp fifty-dollar bill. There went his tithe for the week. "And tell me if you need more."

Who had the upper hand now that the transaction was complete? Faith be damned; after all, it was his money to spend as he pleased. Was it on behalf of the Devil or God that he promised to serve? Once he ministered for the King of Kings and Lord of Lords. Now a dancing whore was the queen of his soul, and she ruled from a tall, ugly throne at Babe's. She would take everything he had if he gave it. Ashley's fee was the price of his soul. The money felt good in her hand.

Suddenly, the clean-up began. Her interest in him fled like a wounded stray dog. Innocence was no more. In an instant he was changed forever by his encounter with a lovely coed-turned-stripper at Babe's. As a guiltless child she rarely missed Sunday School. Her father was head deacon before his death in a speeding car. She was practically born in a pew. Her parents tithed every week. They sat together on the third row each Sunday. Her devoted mother did her part and that should have been enough. And, moreover, she had just tasted a small slice of Heaven with one of the blood-bought saints who served at the feet of the only living God. What else was a horny Tri Delt to do?

They made their way to a small patio under the moonless southern sky. "Thanks for coming," Ashley said. Her lips were moist and smooth. Brother Jimmy did not answer. He had forgotten why he came. Their parting was bitter-sweet. He tasted the sour guilt which follows the utter bliss of a carnal act. Alas, his turn came and went. He was every man smitten with mortal guilt. There was nothing new under the sun.

The Devil was a cunning little reptile and her name was Ashley White.

VIII

I am worse than the prodigal son.

Brother Jimmy lay alone on his bed in the dark. But there was no one to whom he could run for a feast–no fatted calf awaiting innocent slaughter, no precious gem to enthrall a casual look, no earthly father to rapture a drifting heart and welcome him home with open arms despite his self-destruction. The encounter cost him his soul.

"Oh God," the preacher said as he held his face in his hands. The Lord was always accessible. His touch was never more than a whisper away.

Brother Jimmy passed the night without sleeping at all. An early summer storm brewed in the west, and all over a little Southern town the sky was pitch black. The darkest night was just before dawn.

I am damned to eternal Hell.

He lay paralyzed in the belly of the beast. A flicker of lightening stopped a squirrel in the midst of his cautious sprint. The whole sky roared with contempt. Brother Jimmy froze with regret. Ashley had touched him just right–no, *wrong*. Guilt tugged in the center of his chest. "Father, if it be thy will . . . ." His entire body ached with worry. "Only not my will, but thine be done."

He saw the dancing whore on stage at her second home in the pit of Hell. The scene was forever etched in his mind–a showcase of pussies lit up the stage in Memphis primetime, painted faces with their high pointy cheeks, glittered chests covered with see-through silk nighties, the impressive raw talent of a sexy coed stripping by the pole center stage.

Vanilla extract was on his hands, the smell of cocoa butter in his nose. Ashley's Tri Delta form was completely naked in the lighted display. She flaunted her body this way and that, then stepped into a shuffle with a move that was hotter than Hell. Brother Jimmy saw the pointy nipples again in his mind, the soft white powder cased to a juicy upper lip. He could not let go of the way she made him feel.

The preacher paced back and forth by his bed. Where could he turn after the fall? He sat in a chair, feeling its arms to guide him down.

I am a preacher. How can a self-proclaimed man of God act this way?

He stood by a bookcase and paced back and forth. Brother Jimmy's heart sank with grief. He knelt by his bed, then furtively he whispered the recurring prayer: "Father, if it be thy will, let this yoke pass from me. Only not my will, Lord, but thine be done."

I could use some fresh air, he thought as he arose.

He still had a sermon to write. A simple wooden cross was hammered to the wall near a bookcase next to his dresser, and near it hung a faded picture of the crucified Christ. A single crack in the yellow-cut glass divided the scourged deity, separating not only man but also holy God. He was the image people saw when they yearned for salvation. His were the eyes sinners looked into when they petitioned an earnest prayer. His voice echoed in many an empty soul during restless nights as they tried to forget their worries about family and work. Brother Jimmy's loving arms received men and women who were broken by sin. His sermons lingered in their hearts for days. If he was a savior, then so was his Christ. If he was a phony, so was his God.

Brother Jimmy stood quietly by his desk. “Oh God,” he whispered. “I am damned to eternal Hell.” He clasped his hands and covered his guilty face.

He was as dead as the perverts lurking at Babe’s.

PART FOUR

AFTER THE FALL

I

Faith, it seemed, was a forgotten craze. Brother Jimmy remembered his first encounter at Babe's–a drummer rolling hard with his sticks moving quicker as the night wore on, a grown man's eager face splattered with lust, the full frontal nudity in the spotlight at center stage.

"Oh, God." His hands were moist. He yearned for a cheap whore's erotic embrace. She robbed him of what he loved most about her, what intrigued him both night and day since the time he had guessed her age at Browning. He marveled at what might be until he saw her hard at work–the way she walked on stage in the nude and climbed on the pole while music played overhead, how she looked from behind in a tiny silk thong, the way she moved and felt in his lap in the little corner slot of the VIP where the lights were dim. Alas, the allurement of wonder took shape before his eyes as she walked tall on the Memphis stage and tantalized lost souls who stood in line awaiting the imminent thrill. But the tender nudge from his enlivened conscience drew him back home. The day was calm. The church was still. There was nothing to do except pray for forgiveness, for peace, and the strength to get on with the simple life and message he was ordained to preach.

He walked into the kitchen and poured a glass of tea. A locomotive blew its imposing horn as it passed by the abandoned depot just down the street. The preacher swished the tea in his mouth as he paced back and forth in front of the sink. He took another sip, then sat in a chair. His mind raced again with the indelible shame that was his own.

Brother Jimmy cried with his eyes tightly closed. *How can I preach like this*? A small round clock on the wall made its quiet familiar noise. He watched the second hand as it clicked past four. "Almost morning," he thought, "the sun will be up soon."

Brother Jimmy walked slowly up the incline on his way to the church. He still had a sermon to write.

II

Weeks passed and still his guilt remained. He spent more time in his office. "Father, if it be thy will, let this burden pass from me." The preacher's face ached with a shame he had never known. The *Holy Bible* lay closed on his desk. "Only not my will, but . . . ." He heard a gentle knock on the door.

"Brother Jimmy?" The muffled sound came from a young woman's familiar lips. "Are you there?" she asked. He stood and walked quickly toward the door, flinging it open to see the pretty face whose voice he had heard.

"I'm pregnant," Ashley said.

He grabbed her arm and led her to a chair.

"What? Are you sure?" he said with an expression of disbelief.

"I took three tests and all were positive," Ashley said. She held a Bible close to her chest.

Brother Jimmy leaned back in his chair. His face was still; his eyes were cold.

For by means of a whorish woman a man is brought low.

"Now what?" he asked.

"We could get married."

But what would his congregation think? What would Judge Peters say? Would he be forced to resign or permitted to keep the church if he saved face with a simple marriage vow?

He paced back and forth, then sat at his desk. His office chair squeaked with each turn of his nervous hips. The preacher's face turned pale from a fear he had never felt. His eyes retreated with the shame in his head. Brother Jimmy reached for a wad of cash in the offering plate underneath his desk. "Here, take this," he said sternly, giving her a wad of cash. "Do what you have to do."

The young woman kissed his cheek, then turned and reached for the door.

"My sin is worse than death," he confessed to himself. "I am worse than the prodigal son, a pariah." His heart oozed with regret. His palms were moist with shame. "I am not merely avoided," he whispered. "I am despised."

Obedience could set him free. The preacher

knelt at the side of his desk. He thought of the pretty face and young perky breasts, the firm nipples pointing out at him next to the stage, the smooth tan legs that looked just as they should. His forehead dripped with sweat from a lustful thought he could not put away. His member stirred. The memory of sex was in his flesh, his bones. He thrust frantically back and forth, pretending to be inside Ashley again. "I am in love with a whore," he confessed in his heart, "and now I have killed my child."

III

A plaid quilt sewn by his late grandmother covered a single white cotton sheet where he lay on his bed. "Oh God," he prayed, "let this burden pass from me." The preacher recalled his wife's caring words: "That poor girl. She's so cute. I wish she could live with us. Oh, God, you sent us grace. Give it to her, too. May she know your peace."

He pulled back on a dresser drawer to retrieve his wife's diary. It lay by a rusty revolver that had not been fired in years.

It's just for self-defense.

He felt the cold metal with the palm of his hand. Every Southern man keeps a gun in his house, even a simple Baptist preacher who has no enemies save himself. A lone bullet was left in the case. Brother Jimmy inspected its tip.

He opened his wife's diary and reached for a pen. His mind was still as he remembered her face. The sun beamed through his bedroom window and glistened sharply on his face.

"I am sorry for letting you down in the worst

possible way, for defiling the daughter you never had but always treated as your own."

IV

Brother Jimmy left the parsonage and walked slowly up an incline on Reynolds Street at sunset. The clear windows of a shoe store drew his eyes to the right. A young store clerk turned over a sign on the other side of the glass door: *Closed.* He stopped and looked at a row of expensive dress shoes on the lighted display.

Suddenly his head deacon rounded the street corner in a jet-black coupe built for speed.

"Did you have a good time in Memphis?" Judge Peters asked as he stopped and rolled a window down. Brother Jimmy froze with surprise.

"Don't worry, preacher," the judge said curtly. "I've been there, too. Your secret is safe with me."

The judge grinned and squealed his tires and sped down the hill.

It was then he realized that his life had changed. He was hired to fill the void left after another minister's turbulent departure amidst controversy surrounding an alleged affair with the church secretary. The young preacher took charge in the middle of a costly building project that was his predecessor's seemingly good idea. But poor planning and lack of funds gave rise to financial hardship, producing an emotional milieu just right for the tumultuous scandal that ensued between the prior reverend and his assistant. The flock desperately needed a new shepherd, someone they could count on through thick and thin.

The search committee made an appearance one morning in the small country church Brother Jimmy pastored with pride after finishing seminary. They urged him to consider a move and return to a special place called home.

His trial sermon was fitly said. He had penned it in one sitting with ease. Brother Jimmy impressed his audience with the bold message he delivered, awed with the smooth words from his tongue. The preacher was nimble and fair. He called for a truce and the church's internal conflict abated. Brother Jimmy promised to practice as he preached.

The warm reception he enjoyed a few years back would be undone if his shameful sins were ever exposed. His proclaimed integrity would become a blatant lie.

V

Ashley's mind was frozen, unable to decide. She drove east on Lamar, then pulled into a parking lot by an abandoned store. Her mind expanded with the possibility of what her life could be, to the prospect of being a loving mother, of having a powerless child to raise by herself, and the promise of becoming the woman she had always wanted to be. Her head throbbed with the pain of her heart's toughest decision. She had no mother to lean on who would understand, no preacher to count on for needed prayer. Ashley sobbed at the disappointment that had become the habitual practice of her tragic life.

She needed someone to confide in, a handler, someone who had been there, a woman familiar with hardship and who knew the hurt she felt. Who could advise her about what to do? Diamond was the best listener Ashley knew–patient, objective, smart. Cherry was younger and had made all the mistakes unfortunate women usually commit. Hell, they had both been knocked up, too.

"It's hard for a single mom these days," Cherry said.

"Always has been," Diamond agreed. "But I don't know, Ashley. Do what you want to do. It's your body."

"I know," Ashley said, "I just don't understand." She cried again while the girls hugged her in a corner of the dressing room.

"Wait," Diamond said, "How did he take the news?"

Ashley's forehead wrinkled slightly. "Not well," she said as she sobbed and wiped her cheek, "He just reached for a stack of bills in the offering plate and then led me to the door."

"Uh! How could a minister fund an abortion?" Diamond asked with a look of dismay.

"That bastard!" Cherry said, "and with the donations of hard-working people."

"He's probably just as shocked as you are," the older stripper said. "Give him a few days. He may change his mind."

Ashley thought, *How could he tell a helpless young woman to kill an innocent baby?* Once he took an oath to have other people's salvation first on his mind, but now he was preoccupied with the termination of his son or daughter's budding life.

"Think about yourself, Ashley," Cherry said. "You have the rest of your life to live. It's no more involved than changing a dirty tampon. Plus, it's done by a doctor in a special room."

Diamond sat quietly next to Ashley on the wooden bench. She showed a subtle disdain for Cherry's hasty advice.

"Listen, honey. Live your dream," Cherry said, "You only live once." She had a look of authority about her face. "You can be anything you want." She stroked Ashley's hair to one side. "You don't need some nagging rug rat grabbing at your ankles all the time, holding you back. God knows, men will run from you. You're smart. Why don't you get your nursing degree and work in a hospital? You'll be glad you listened to me," Cherry ranted, shaking her finger in Ashley's face. "Hell, with your looks you might even marry a fucking doctor like my sister did."

"Thanks, girls," Ashley said as she fumbled for a tissue in her purse, "Y'all are great."

Days passed. She waited for an answer in the form of a sign from the holy God she barely knew. She waited for more tears, but they did not come.

I can't cry anymore, Ashley thought, *I have to be strong and decide what to do.*

VI

The preacher sat in the back of the room while his head deacon presided over court. *Circuit Judge Charles Peters* read the name plate secured next to a wooden gavel. The judge reigned from his throne like a cogent lower deity. He peered over small bifocals, making note of the preacher seated in the last row of the courtroom. The air had a faint smell of cedar. The sprawling inscription on the wall above the judge's seat etched a permanent place in the pastor's mind: *To Thine Own Self Be True.*

God slams his righteous gavel to rule on whether vulnerable souls are lost or saved, Brother Jimmy thought. His heart beat with shame. With his sweaty hands and tremulous lips, anyone could see he looked disturbed–tainted by a past he could not undo, weary from the unshakable guilt of a lustful act. Sex was supposed to be light and fun, but now his mind was riddled with guilt. A slogan on the state seal caught his eye: *Virtute et armis.*

"I have no valor or virtue in which to trust," Brother Jimmy muttered to himself. A divorce hearing proceeded before him. The preacher sank with the burden in his heart. His face was unsettled and tense. A preacher, a judge: Who else had fallen victim to the little dancing whore?

The two men left the courtroom together. Judge Peters jiggled a few coins in his pants pocket.

"The timeless lessons of life are best explained from a Broadway stage or a classic work of English lit," Judge Peters said in his chamber. "Think of Orwell and Wilde," he continued as he lit a pipe: "Have we sunk to such a depth that the restatement of the obvious has become the duty of intelligent men?" The judge turned to hang up his robe, laying his pipe by the vanity mirror. A soft plume of smoke from fresh burning tobacco rose in the musty air. Judge Peters said, "The inverse of a welcome probability will generally present itself at a time when it is most likely to be frustrating."

Brother Jimmy was quiet and still. A statue of Lady Justice rested on the vanity. The preacher glared at her sword and scales. *A symbol of moral force*, he thought. *My soul hangs in the balance.* He sat gingerly in a chair. The preacher listened skeptically with wide, hungry eyes.

"Small problems become big problems when they are ignored long enough," Judge Peters said. Brother Jimmy's soul hung on every word. "You counsel others to walk the straight and narrow, but do not practice what you preach." The judge placed both hands on his desk. "Jim, I think it's time you stepped down."

The preacher's face turned pale.

"Don't worry. You'll be fine," Judge Peters said. "This was your first real job out of seminary. I'm sure another church will call."

Brother Jimmy did not answer.

"Just remember," the head deacon went on, "the truth is often inconvenient and sometimes embarrassing, but must be illuminated in spite of circumstance–if not in this life, then perhaps in the one to come." Judge Peters blew a puff of smoke from the pipe he savored like his favorite scotch. "She got loose in my pants, too, you know," Judge Peters said. "I had no idea she would get loose in yours."

Brother Jimmy listened as a wayward child. His eyes were clear and still.

"But you are a preacher and I am not. Just do what you can to make it right.

"Truth," the judge said as he propped his feet on the dark wooden desk while smoking his hand-crafted pipe, "has an illuminating quality all its own. Perceptions are all that count to the simple, but never mind them–the truth is really all that matters."

Brother Jimmy pushed open the huge front door of the courthouse. He was left with a decision no man should have to make: To carry on with a broken spirit in the spotlight of public shame or accept the painful and immutable truth that his pastoral life was suddenly over. His part in attempting to save a wayward soul had somehow cost him his own.

The door of the austere courthouse closed firmly behind him. The noise echoed down a vacant hall and past the jury room that heard every excuse a man could invent. Brother Jimmy trudged back to his house. He lowered his head feebly as he took the first steps home. The wise admonition flashed again in his head: *To Thine Own Self Be True.*

A church bell rang boldly through the vacant streets in town.

VII

"Feet in the stirrups, honey. The doctor will be in soon."

"Okay," Ashley said as she repositioned the pristine sheet over her knees. A woman's voice screamed bloody murder from a room down the hall.

The door opened again. "Are you sure you want to do this, hon'?" The nurse stared at her subject blankly.

Ashley focused on a tiny speck in the ceiling. She remembered her mother's face.

"Do you need some time to think about it?" the nurse asked.

"No, I'm ready," she said with apparent resolve. The hasty decision seemed incredibly intimate.

"Okay. I'll let the doctor know," the nurse said as she closed the door.

Maybe Cherry was right. Maybe her dreams would come true. But what if she never conceived again? What if she killed her only child?

The maternal instinct is powerful and fierce. Women are made to breed. The birth of a child is a permanent, life-altering event. Pregnancy may be hard, but the temporary inconvenience pays off in the end. If her pregnancy continued, she would feel the baby move inside her body; the unborn life was already part of her. Being with child was a strange and uncomfortable state, but she could get use to it.

Last week she danced by a pole. Yesterday she took money from a Baptist preacher with no problem at all. A few moments before, she signed in at the clinic where she had come for help. But somehow her apathy toward the unborn had turned into abiding concern. Ashley's heart was transformed. Her soul was imbued with hope. The young woman felt an urgent need to move. Her uncertainty cleared as quickly as it developed. Ashley's mind was clear. No more lap dances, no more tricks. No more Babe's or shining lights. No more smoke-filled room, no more crumpled wads of dirty cash. Her chest would be free of glitter. She had spun for the last time on the brass pole at center stage. The stripper was done with the frantic show and now she would follow her dream.

Time was the resource she could least afford to lose. Brother Jimmy needed to hear her good news. She was not carrying a pointless glob of tissue–she was pregnant with a human life.

VIII

The service continued with Mr. White's earnest prayer. He looked at the preacher, then bowed his head:

Our Father, which art in Heaven,
Hallowed be thy name
Thy kingdom come; Thy will be done
In earth as it is in Heaven.
Give us this day our daily bread
And forgive us our trespasses,
As we forgive those who trespass against us.
And lead us not into temptation;
But deliver us from evil.
For thine is the kingdom,
And the power, and the glory,
Forever and ever,
Amen.

Brother Jimmy planted his hands on the pulpit and looked at the congregants staring back at him from every pew. A wrinkle on his forehead grew deeper as the moments passed, but his sermon's central message was plainly stated. Brother Jimmy closed with a poem. Ashley heard the most important lines:

The love of God is greater far
Than tongue or pen can ever tell.
It goes beyond the highest star,
And reaches to the lowest hell.

Oh, love of God, how rich and pure!
How measureless and strong!
It shall forevermore endure

the saints and angels song.
Could we with ink the ocean fill,
And were the skies of parchment made,
Were every stalk on earth a quill,
And every man a scribe by trade;
To write the love of God above
Would drain the ocean dry;
Nor could the scroll contain the whole,
Though stretched from sky to sky!

The organist played the first verse of the invitation hymn. Her shoes reminded one of a pilgrim. Brother Jimmy's prayer continued as earnestly as it began. "God is unwavering in His love. In spite of our most wicked sin, Christ died for us. Forsaking Himself, He meets us wherever we are and no matter what we have done. Why? Because of grace. Amazing Grace."

Brother Jimmy bowed his head and said: "It is very meet and right, and our bounden duty, that we should at all times, and in all places, give thanks unto thee, O Lord, holy Father, almighty, everlasting God. For thou didst die a cruel death on a Roman cross to save us from our worst sins."

A strange feeling came to Ashley's chest as she left the crowded pew. There was a hint of conviction on her face. The certain mood of salvation stirred in her heart and soul.

"Praise God!" Brother Jimmy exclaimed when the hymn was over. "Another sinner has just been saved!" Ashley stood with both hands behind her waist. She beamed her smile with a perfect face.

"When do you want to be baptized?" the preacher asked.

"Today," the young woman said. The congregation nodded and smiled in unison.

"Amen!" one of the deacons said.

Brother Jimmy whispered something in the young woman's ear. She nodded affectionately as the preacher raised her hand with his lanky arm.

"Ashley White will be baptized in Longview Creek this afternoon at 3:00 p.m.," the preacher said. "Beloved, another sinner just came home."

The sun cast its first ray of hope over the narrow streets in town.

IX

A thin crowd gathered along the creek bank as preacher and sinner took off their shoes. They stood on dark red clay that turned into mud when pressed under the murky water by their bare feet. Ashley White donned a white cotton gown. A school of tadpoles swam slowly by her feet.

Her tired grandfather watched as he leaned against the trunk of a huge oak tree. A whiff of fresh honeysuckle breezed by the old man's nose. Two happy squirrels scurried on a limb, then leaped to the solid trunk. Empty shells of acorns were scattered on the ground. A covey of songbirds squawked a gentle prelude. The sound was sweet in the midst of nature's quiet repose.

Ashley scanned the creek bank with the busy eyes of a weary traveler who has just arrived home. The smell of cocoa butter was still in her nose. She thought of a dance move that earned good pay, the tall stack of cash seized from eager looks, then crammed tightly into a fashionable purse when her work was done at Babe's. Was she ready for a permanent change?

She grabbed the preacher's flexed bicep to

break her fall. The congregants gasped, then exhaled together in an expression of relief. The cool water in Longview Creek was still. A few parishioners gathered round.

"Buried with Christ in baptism," Brother Jimmy said as he dunked the sexy sinner into the muddy creek, "and raised to walk in newness of life."

Dusk fell on the quiet little town. The setting sun cast its last warm rays on the magnolias in the stately court square. A long shadow moved like a lazy dial over the bold rebel soldier lofted high in the center of town. The air turned cool as a pretty sunset came and went, and all over the peaceful, sober land a good night's rest was not far behind.

X

Mr. White shut the door of his red brick shed and looked toward the sky. The sun hung low, beaming once more over the cemetery not far from town. The old man looked contentedly at the garden he had made, then walked into his house.

"Almost time," he sighed as he wiped his heavy brow. "Won't be long."

A great-horned owl stood calmly on a huge oak's top limb, eyeing a young hare lost from its fold. The hardy bird gave its traditional call: "Hoo hoo hoo, hoo hoo hoo."

Clarence White closed his eyes for what would be his final rest. The bedroom was silent, except for the tick, tick, tick of an antique clock. The Baptist church was quiet; its stained-glass windows gleamed in radiant glory. A lone, aged sparrow looked down from the roof, queuing a chorus of crickets. The court square was empty. A gentle wind stirred a magnolia in the center of town. Another soul had moved on.

The church bells in town clanged beautifully again.

XI

Brother Jimmy's most private sin was rumored all over town. Dirty gossip sustains and renews. It filled the boredom of an indolent Monday afternoon with purpose and laughs and tears. The preacher was left to brood alone. He could not put away from his mind the sins he had thought and done. His heartbeat was weak and slow as he sat alone on his bed.

His lips quivered slightly as his small hand lifted the gun to the side of his head. His mind flashed a picture of the small-town girl touched by good looks who carried his only child, at least for a while. In an instant, life was irrevocably changed for both of them. He thought of the sanctuary where he was paid to preach: the quiet baptismal and hefty pulpit, twin stained-glass windows with their grand pictures of the resurrected Christ, arms open and ready for loving embrace, the handsome Jesus draped with his brilliant robe and cradling a helpless lamb that was lost from its fold. He remembered his mother's unconditional love, the delicate touch of her hands that nurtured him from the crib.

Brother Jimmy considered the grief in his

heart as he sat alone in silence: "The Good Shepherd looks after his sheep."

Slowly, deliberately, he squeezed the trigger. Blood spurted from his temple onto a sheetrock wall. The crimson liquid trickled to the floor, then beside the errant preacher in whom it still flowed as he lay fighting for his tattered life. The dead Christ was splattered with blood, but the tearful confession left him clean. A crumpled piece of paper lay on the *Holy Bible.* Scribbled hurriedly in bold red letters:

"I needed to die."

Word of the preacher's mortal sin spread like a virus. Doctor Rayburn responded when called; the head deacon did the same. Jimmy Russell's body froze like the snapshot of a fallen soldier whose bravery was rewarded contemptuously with the tragedy of untimely death. The thick Southern air joined with solemnity, purged of sinful intrigue that lay bare the muted soul of a humble man whose unholy struggle was the heart of life itself.

Doctor Rayburn reached for the preacher's wrist and felt a feeble pulse. He repositioned his finger again. Was it his own pulse that he was feeling? No, it was the preacher's. Brother Jimmy's heart was still beating. The preacher was still alive.

The sun hung low, then eased slowly out of sight, and all over the little town the faithful few mourned for the soul of their wayward yet earnest preacher who lay immersed in sorrow at close of day. A covey of birds alighted from the post office roof a block from the church. The magnolias stood proud as a brave rebel soldier kept watch over the majestic court square and the sleepy streets of town.

No one heard the crack of the gun, save a small child playing near an empty street.

XII

The sign in the beauty shop window read, *Sorry, We're Closed*, at the end of day. The two stylists who worked there quietly cleaned their mutual space. A woman with a serious expression reached for a dust pan and broom. The other knelt to wipe off her chair.

"They baptized Ashley White in Longview Creek last Sunday," the older one said. "I reckon Satan's lost his right-hand gal."

"She's finally made a turn to the Lord after stripping all those years," the junior stylist said. "I heard Brother Jimmy did the dunking."

"He did. It was the day before he shot himself."

"Reckon that was on account of something him and Ashley did?"

"Hell if I know. I heard he went to Memphis and witnessed to her. I wouldn't be surprised, though, not around here. I'm just glad Mr. White lived to see her get saved."

"She had to live somehow, but I just can't see stripping all those years. Not me, honey, no ma'am. These iron panties are hard to pull down."

"Since she's quit dancing, I really don't know what she's done. And, girl, let me tell you–it costs money to look that good."

"You should have seen her after she got her

hair done when we were in school. And for no less than twenty-five dollars, I might add."

"Cost a lot to cover them horns."

"Yep, and that was years ago. Probably runs her twice that much now."

The church bells rang softly as the setting sun moved further away.

XIII

She drove northwest on Lamar, past a Boot Corral and a run-down Oil and Lube across from a deserted package store. A man with a blue-collared shirt displaying his name on the front gave a half-hearted wave when he saw Ashley's face for a moment as she sped by. She looked at him in the mirror while holding onto the wheel with one hand and with a lone finger caressed her sleeping son on the cheek. The baby rested peacefully despite their ride on the bumpy road.

They came to a stop in front of a traffic light during rush hour at the intersection of Winchester and Lamar. A vagrant with a haggard beard held a cardboard sign with both hands directly above his head. The sign had only one word: *Jesus*. The man looked vaguely familiar. He was missing one eye and part of his nose. "Jesus saves!" the man cried as he lurched on a sidewalk by the busy road, holding his sign close to each windshield for the commuters to see.

"Repent! Repent, I say! Repent for the kingdom of Heaven is near!"

Ashley stared at the man with a look of concern. She parked her car on one side of the road. “Brother Jimmy? Is that you?” she said as she approached the man. The familiar man dodged a car as he limped onto the street. Ashley’s eyes held a worried expression as she noticed his twisted face. The man turned his head to hide a long scar on his forehead; the face was a distortion of one she had admired before.

“Preacher, is that you?” She offered him a kerchief as a gesture of kindness. “Do you need a ride home?” she asked. His hands were thin and wasted. The bony knuckles shown through his malnourished skin. He had no soft place to lay his head. The man’s eyes held the nervous gaze of a hungry drifter forced to live outdoors.

“Home is where your feet are,” he mumbled without emotion.

Ashley cradled her new son as the hideous looking man turned away. She thought of the innocent pastor on whose heart she had preyed. Then her eyes fell on the child whose life she had made with the man who still preached despite his distorted face.

XIV

Morning arrived too soon. Ashley awoke in a haze to a sweaty man beside her sleeping like a hog in the summer sun. A cute babe touched her face as though causing the sun to rise. She threw warm covers over her head and pleaded for peace. The baby’s hungry whimper did not go away. The sun’s early light slowly filled the room. Breakfast was a piece of toast and jelly. Eating was an involuntary task, a necessity if life were to go on. She was not the volunteering kind. A tramp swallows without thinking, not wanting to clean up. There was never enough time.

Sadness washed away like a working girl's cheap mascara. A late October sun peaked in the southern sky. Dark clouds hovered in the east. Ashley White rocked her new babe on the front porch swing. The radio played a country song. A sonorous voice sounded like Paul Thorn.

Down at the Baptist Sunday school board
I work stacking Bibles from seven to four.
I guess the will of God has got to be obeyed,
But I know I wouldn't do it if I didn't get paid.
Amen.

Her new man sat roughly and spit in a cup. He held a can of snuff with one hand and with the other popped open a beer.

"What time did you get in last night?" he asked.

Let it go, she thought. *Your head is pounding enough from the hangover. Just be quiet.* She opened a pack of Marlboros and swatted a lazy fly. *You can lose a battle and still win the war.* The young woman missed and tried again.

A cool breeze refreshed like incense in the cathedral of nature. The insect flew away.

"Can you keep the baby tonight?" Ashley asked. "I have to work."

EPILOGUE

Brother Jimmy is alive today. He still preaches to lost souls who wonder forgotten streets in Memphis. The magnolia in our front yard still stands proud as another little boy sits on its highest limb to keep watch with a brave rebel soldier over the sleepy court square and the narrow streets of town.

Starner Jones, MD is a board-certified emergency medicine physician. Born and raised in the rural hill country of northeast Mississippi, he was educated at the University of the South in Sewanee, Tennessee, and Saint George's University School of Medicine. He is a recent graduate of the Emergency Medicine Residency Program at The University of Mississippi Medical Center. In addition to reading works by his favorite author, Graham Greene, Jones enjoys world travel, hunting, fishing, and playing golf. He lives alone in Memphis.